"Are you here to seduce me?"

The husky timbre of Matt's voice stroked her jangled nerves. Kassidy was startled by the need that burned in his eyes.

"Is that why you came, Kass? You want to make love?"

Kassidy was tempted. Making love meant she could show him with her body how well suited they were. Instead, she plunged ahead. "I was planning to propose marriage to you first."

"Marriage?" Matt frowned.

Kassidy was confused and afraid. "When we made love last week . . . I thought . . ."

"One night of great sex and you're ready to jump back into that hellhole we called a marriage—"

"What we have together is more than great sex!" Kassidy was infuriated. What did the man want from her?

"Nothing's changed between us. Getting married again would only be disastrous." Matt studied her pale face intently. He was taking the biggest gamble of his life. "Until you figure out what went wrong between us . . . the answer is no."

Dear Reader,

Talk about writing from a position of inexperience—or so I thought last year when my editor asked me to explore the lives of two seemingly incompatible lovers. Using my own marriage as a model certainly wouldn't work. After all, you'd never find two more compatible people than my husband and I.

Nevertheless, I sat down and listed our likes and dislikes, waiting for the obvious parallels to overwhelm me. Yes, I know you've figured out the punch line, but frankly the exercise was truly an eye-opener for me. Not only should we *not* be married, I wondered how we'd even managed to coexist on the same planet!

But we *are* married, and happily I might add. Compromise snuck up on us when we weren't looking. In *Détente*, the necessity for it slaps Kassidy and Matt in the face. Their struggles give us insight into the process of building a lasting relationship that is based on giving, sharing and loving.

Happy reading!
Emma Jane Spenser

Détente

EMMA JANE SPENSER

Harlequin Books

TORONTO • NEW YORK • LONDON
AMSTERDAM • PARIS • SYDNEY • HAMBURG
STOCKHOLM • ATHENS • TOKYO • MILAN

Published February 1991

ISBN 0-373-25436-9

DÉTENTE

Prologue

"I GUESS WE LEAPED before we looked."

Kassidy grimaced at the regret in Matt's voice, then nodded in agreement. "That'll teach us," she said with a sigh, looking at the man she'd just divorced. No Contest, the clerk had noted on the papers as he'd mumbled something about the ninety-day waiting period. But to Kassidy that was nothing more than a technicality. The divorce was every bit as real today as it would be three months from now. "You'd think two intelligent people would have seen it coming."

He shook his head slowly, the self-disparaging half grin drawing her gaze away from the hurt in his eyes. It was his mouth that she'd miss most, she thought, swallowing hard to keep the emotion from spilling out of her eyes. Or perhaps the silly grin that invited her to play when she was too busy, those hard lips that made her forget everything else.

More than once she'd allowed herself to be seduced away from work. Matt had seen her all-consuming drive as a challenge to be overcome, interrupting her whirlwind schedule with a whispered, lascivious suggestion... the promise of heaven in his arms. There were whole afternoons when she'd played hooky just to be with him, hours that should have been spent with an eye to the future.

With Matt her life had stalled. Their six months together hadn't been much time according to a calendar, but Kassidy measured things differently—by the promotion that should have been hers and wasn't.

It was time to get on with her life and her plans. This— their divorce—was the first step.

Kassidy looked at Matt, grateful his gaze was directed out the window. It didn't make things any easier to know he still loved her. Just as she still loved him. She swallowed again as her eyes carefully traced the familiar lines of his face.

Unfortunately, love hadn't been enough. Their constant bickering and daily battles had finally broken down the will to live together.

Not all of the battles had been big, not all of the bickering pointless. But in the end, the sheer number of opportunities for confrontation had eventually overwhelmed them. They'd argued about everything from food to the kind of sheets they preferred on the bed.

Kassidy broke the backs of every paperback book she picked up, while Matt treated each one as a treasure to be preserved.

She thrived on junk food and leftovers. He ate health food.

He was a slob. She wasn't.

And so on. Kassidy scowled at the petty reminders of her own paralytic resistance to change, wondering how those silly differences had grown into such ridiculous arguments. But they'd only been symptoms of the bigger things.

Things like her career, and his inattention to his own.

Things like money. Not the lack of it, but how to spend it. Or how not to spend it, she corrected herself. Matt spent every penny he had on whatever caught his fancy. Kassidy didn't spend a dime without a good reason.

Not all their differences took the form of arguments. To look at the two of them was to wonder about the adage that opposites attract.

He was tall—a couple of inches over six feet, blonde, athletic and tan. In a word, rugged.

She was short—about five feet four inches on a good day. Her hair was jet black and curly, deliberately tamed to smooth, sophisticated waves for the office. She wasn't athletic, and therefore not tanned. Delicate was how Matt used to describe her. And she'd argue, because there was nothing delicate about her approach to business, but he'd say that wasn't what he was talking about. She looked delicate, he'd correct himself.

They were as opposite as their names. She was Canyon. He was Hill.

At times, it seemed the only thing they had in common was their age—thirty-two.

After six months of marriage, the pain of their battles had finally taken its toll.

And now, with the divorce papers properly signed, filed and served, Kassidy Canyon and Matt Hill were no longer married. Essentially not married, she amended, realizing there was a waiting period, but knowing it added no meaning to what they'd just done.

So why was she sitting here with Matt in a coffee shop, instead of at her desk where she belonged?

"How soon do you close on the condominium?"

He startled her, asking such a practical question. That wasn't like him at all.

"Next week. But I can move my things in anytime," she told him, wishing the details weren't so painful. "They've set up a temporary rental agreement until the sale goes through."

"Need any help?" He cleared something hard from his throat, wanting to take back the offer, but knowing there wasn't any point. She wouldn't accept help from him, not today.

"I've already arranged everything," she said. "And I'm not taking anything from our house—your house—that I can't carry myself."

"You can have anything you want," he said, surprising her by reaching across the table to touch her hand. "You know that, don't you?"

She almost lost it then, almost cried when she needed to be strong. It was his warmth that did it, the pinpoints of heat that pulsed from his fingertips to the back of her hand. Her reaction to his silly grin made her wonder if they were doing the right thing.

"I know that," she finally managed to say, and with a deep breath for courage, pulled her hand away from the familiar comfort of his. "But the condo is rather modern, and none of our stuff exactly fits." Not that she'd take it, anyway, not with the memories of their loving branded on every chair and table. Well, not *every* chair and table, she conceded, feeling the first smile in a long time edging her lips upward.

"What's so funny?" he asked, leaning back with his arms crossed over his chest. It wasn't a defensive position, she knew. Matt didn't need body language to express himself. He had always been incredibly open about his feelings, letting her know how much he loved her, and later, how he thought things were changing.

Because things had changed, she remembered. Not the love. No, that had always been there. But it had somehow gotten buried under the rubbish of their lives, the little things that had pushed them apart, until the love they shared was no longer strong enough to hold them together.

She loved him but she couldn't live with him.

"I asked you what you were laughing at," he repeated, watching her amusement change to sadness. He hated to see that painful expression on her face, but knew there was little he could do to change it.

"I don't remember." Wouldn't remember, she decided, suddenly wanting to get this over. Checking her watch as though she had somewhere to be, she attempted a lighter mood. "Seems a shame that it takes three whole months to dissolve a marriage that only lasted six."

"You in a hurry?"

"Only to get back to the office." She sidestepped the question with a response he was used to, praying that this day would soon be over, and her life could get back to normal. "And you?"

He grinned, admiring her determination to keep everything on an even keel. "I'm going to the mountains for a week or so. Thought I'd get in some fishing and hiking before Roger ties me back to the desk."

"Roger never ties you to the desk," she retorted, relieved to have the conversation on a level she could handle. "Roger would be happy if you never came into the office."

"But then what would I do with my time?" Lifting the cup for a last taste of coffee, Matt wondered why he baited her like this. It didn't make sense, not when he knew precisely what she'd say in reply.

"Why, you'd just do some more camping and fishing or whatever," she said, rising from her chair under his steady gaze. "Isn't that what makes you happy?"

"If you say so." Oddly disappointed, even though he'd seen the response coming, Matt flowed with it. "In the meantime, be sure and keep in touch about that Girl Scout troop of yours. I've got the campsite and some nice trails picked out."

Kassidy grinned, knowing she was being teased. "I'll be sure and tell Millie. You know she's in charge of the outdoor stuff."

"You mean you're not going?" Feigning surprise, Matt pushed open the cafeteria door and walked alongside her as they headed for the parking lot behind the courthouse.

"Does 'over my dead body' mean anything to you?"

"Seems I've heard it a few times." They'd reached her car, an old sedan with multiple dents and scratches that Kassidy never seemed to notice. Of course, Matt wouldn't be caught dead in her car, preferring instead the late-model Mercedes-Benz that he'd parked in the far corner, away from thoughtless door-dingers.

Risking a final look at the woman beside him, he wondered for the hundredth time why their marriage had gone so wrong. Blue eyes looked up at him, misting with an emotion she couldn't hide as her fingers dragged nervously through the shoulder-length mane of black curls.

She was the woman he loved, but he couldn't live with her. And as it had turned out, she couldn't live with him. They were, in a word, incompatible.

"I'll miss you," she whispered, her eyes filling with the tears that had threatened all morning.

"I'll only be gone a week." He couldn't bring himself to say it was over, not when he still loved her so much.

"Divorce is forever," she said, wondering why she was trying so hard to drive that point home.

"We're still friends," he told her, cupping her chin with one hand as his other pulled out a rumpled handkerchief to wipe away her tears.

"We'll always be friends, you know."

"I know." And because the tears wouldn't stop falling, she tore herself out of his grip and jumped into the car. She didn't look at him, not even through the rearview mirror as she pulled out of the parking lot and plunged into the speeding traffic.

They'd always be friends, she consoled herself. Friends, but never again lovers. Never again husband and wife. Perhaps that was best.

Before Kassidy could decide if she really believed that, her thoughts were interrupted by the shrill summons of the car telephone. Almost grateful, she picked up the receiver.

MATT STARED after the car, noticing the black smoke coming from her muffler as she dived into a break in the traffic. He thought about calling her office and leaving a message to remind her to have it looked at, but knew she'd already have made an appointment—squeezed in between getting her hair cut and a Friends of the Library meeting or whatever.

"Divorce is forever." Swallowing hard as he repeated the words to himself, Matt turned and looked back to the corner where his gleaming red sports coupé was parked.

Perhaps, he admitted reluctantly, still finding it hard to swallow over the lump in his throat. Taking long strides past the rows of cars, he thought about it. *Divorce is forever.*

And perhaps not.

1

KASSIDY SNEEZED with her eyes open.

It wasn't an easy feat, but driving with her eyes closed didn't appeal to her sense of fair play. Even at this late hour there were other cars on the road, and they deserved better than to be run down by a blind sneeze.

She sneezed again, swerving a little this time from the force of it. "Damn that cat!" she swore, wishing she'd had the sense to leave before things had gotten out of control. But she hadn't, naively believing she could survive the night, locked in her own room.

She'd given up the battle at midnight. Leaving a suspiciously unrepentant roommate alone with the feline invader, Kassidy and her allergies had fled the condo.

The mist was heavy, clinging to the windshield and sweeping in through the window she'd left cracked open. Kassidy poked the wiper button, then slammed the heel of her palm down upon it when it didn't obey her first command. Reluctantly, the wiper blades began to stroke across the window.

Perhaps she should call ahead, she mused, feeling for the telephone in the console beside her. But her hand dropped away as she reconsidered. Tactically, calling ahead was a bad move. If she just showed up on his doorstep, he couldn't turn her away.

At least, she didn't think Matt could turn her away.

He would treat her like any other friend and give her a bed for the night. And if he was busy... Well, Kassidy could accept that, too. She was over being hurt, she told herself. Matt's personal life was, well, personal. And she was a mature adult, who merely needed a place to stay for the night.

After all, she reminded herself, it was a year to the day since they'd filed for divorce, nine months since it had become final. And so much had changed since then. She had jumped back onto the fast track at the stockbrokerage, making up for lost time with a determination that felled her competitors. Not one promotion, but two, had come her way, and now she was considering a third. Only considering, because she wasn't sure that moving into a managerial position was what she wanted.

Perhaps change wasn't the proper way to view the last year, she reflected, signaling a right turn. It was more as if things had reverted to the way they were before her marriage. She was charging ahead in her career at full speed, keeping up her involvement with the Girl Scouts and library, as well as other volunteer work. Her days were one hundred percent full, just as they had been before she met Matt.

With him things had been so different. Suddenly there hadn't been room for everything—not if she wanted to keep her marriage together. During the marriage her priorities had not only changed, they'd almost disappeared beneath the loving.

Now she had them back. She had everything back to the way it was before Matt. Even the crease in her finger from her wedding band had long since disappeared. It was as though it had never happened at all.

So why was she so nervous?

Taking a deep, calming breath, Kassidy gingerly pumped the brakes, keeping in mind the rain-slick streets as she approached a red light. If Matt had company, she'd go to her mom's place on the other side of Seattle. On second thought, she rejected that plan. Her sister Tracy and family were visiting, and Tracy would kill her if she woke up the new baby.

It wasn't worth taking the risk.

Her two closest friends, Sarah and Bill, wouldn't do her any good, either. They were in Mazatlán for a long weekend. Wishing they'd chosen a more convenient time to be away, Kassidy reviewed her options.

She rejected the possibility of checking into a hotel. That particular extravagance went against her penny-wise nature. If Matt was busy, she'd just have to sleep in the car.

Kassidy gripped the wheel in preparation for the oncoming sneeze and concentrated on keeping her eyes wide open.

Matt's place was just around the corner.

HE FELT A BIT SILLY sitting in the dark, but knew he couldn't turn on the lights.

She might see them when she drove up...if she drove up. The cat ploy was merely guaranteed to drive her out of her condo. Where she went next was out of his control.

But Matt didn't think she'd drive all the way to her mom's—not at this late hour. Besides, her sister's family was visiting, and beds would be at a premium. There were always friends she could go to, but Matt knew the only two who lived nearby were in Mazatlán. And he was convinced she would never check in at a hotel. Hotels cost money, and that was something Kassidy never parted with easily.

Coming here, to the house they'd once shared, would be a logical thing to do. He shook his head, wondering if logic would work for or against him. With Kassidy he never knew.

He could only hope.

The grandfather clock downstairs had long since struck midnight, and he leaned forward to look through the slit between the bedroom curtains as the echoes faded. Nothing yet. Settling back into the heavy, leather chair that he'd shoved up to the window, Matt prepared to wait a while longer.

He wished he'd asked Marla to call when Kassidy left. At least that way he'd have known when to give it up.

Did Kassidy know this was the precise anniversary of the date they'd filed for divorce? Probably. She didn't usually forget things.

And if she did remember, would that influence her decision? Matt frowned into the black night, wishing he were as sure of her feelings as he was of his own. Knowing he still loved her didn't necessarily mean she still loved him.

He thought she might, if for no other reason than that the love they'd shared had been too intense to evaporate without leaving a trace.

It wasn't as though she'd changed over the year they'd been apart. She was still the same woman he'd married, except that she was considerably more successful without him.

Matt had tried to understand what drove Kassidy to succeed, to be the best. It wasn't success itself, he'd discovered early on, but the fruits of that success. Kassidy wanted security, demanded it, and whatever financial goals she'd set for herself were never enough, once she'd achieved them.

It was because of her parents, she'd told him once, and the lessons she'd learned, growing up in a house where money was scarce, where next month's paycheck was needed to get through today. Hand-to-mouth, she'd said, more frustrated than angry with her parents' lack of financial smarts. There was disbelief, too, that they'd lived their lives without any regard for future security, worrying only when the time came about where they'd get the money for Kassidy's piano lessons, Tracy's braces. They'd always managed, somehow, perhaps sacrificing summer vacation money when an emergency arose . . . taking from Peter to pay Paul.

Not that Kassidy's parents had been poor, Matt knew. They'd just never placed a great deal of importance upon financial planning. Kassidy was determined to live her life differently. As far as Matt could tell, she'd never set a limit on what was enough. That all-consuming drive had extended to all facets of her life, making her a classic Type-A personality as she strove to do as much as she possibly could, and do it all well. She worked like a demon, was active in community activities and then, when she had an extra minute or two, squeezed in a date or another purely social event.

She tried to do it all.

Matt, on the other hand, had no such ambitions. He was a successful businessman, mostly because he'd had a good idea at the right time and in the perfect setting. His sporting goods store boasted booming sales, yet Matt wasn't particularly interested in the business these days. In fact, he'd spent the last twelve months reducing his own participation in favor of a manager, who was now handling almost everything. Free of the day-to-day business concerns, Matt had begun exploring a new career—one that was totally unlike anything he'd previously considered.

He wasn't ready to tell Kassidy, because until he attained a measure of success, he knew she wouldn't understand. Matt shifted in the chair, wondering how long he'd be able to keep up the fiction that he was still working in the store. Fortunately he was still going there regularly, so he supposed it might take a long time before she guessed he'd made some changes.

He'd changed that part of his life, and knew there were other things he'd be only too happy to change, little things that only Kassidy would notice. But it would all be for nothing, unless she came back to him.

If she came back to him.... Matt rose impatiently and began pacing the polished wooden floor of his bedroom. If she came back to him, they could learn to change together.

It wouldn't be easy, but then, it wasn't supposed to be. Wasn't there a saying about having to work hard for something good? Well, he and Kassidy were good together. They just had to learn to get along better.

To change. To compromise.

Matt heard a screech of tires. He was at the window and peering through the opening in the drapes when the car came to a full stop in front of his house, the front tire digging into the soft grass of his lawn.

Kassidy was home.

His relief was almost palpable as he stepped back from the window. He hadn't really expected her to come. He'd hoped for it, even prayed for it, but hadn't truly believed it.

The door bell rang. Glowing in the dark, the hands and numbers of the clock beside the bed told him it was closer to one than midnight.

Tightening the robe around him, Matt flipped on the light and padded barefoot down the stairs. Just in case the robe wasn't adequate proof that he'd been in bed, he ran his fingers through his hair, pulling haphazardly at the dark blond waves until they felt suitably disheveled. The bell pealed again as he threw open the door.

"Atchoo!"

Her sneeze almost blew him off his feet. Matt took cover behind the door, cautiously peering around the edge when no more violent sneezes were forthcoming.

Looking miserable and forlorn, Kassidy blew noisily into a tissue, then stuck a finger beneath her nose in an attempt to ward off another sneeze.

She looked as if she'd been crying, but he knew better and tried to remember that. Kassidy's allergic reactions were never subtle. She made a pathetic picture on his doorstep, huddled inside a thickly quilted coat with the mass of black curls falling every which way, even into her eyes, when she lost the battle with the latest sneeze.

A fresh explosion whipped her head halfway to her knees. Matt was impressed and watched as she prepared herself for another.

She was dressed for anything and everything—the lemon-colored, down coat dropped to her knees, revealing pink knee socks and penny loafers. The frivolous pattern of a flannel nightgown peeked out from the top of the coat, but he knew better than to say anything.

The last time he'd teased her about those old-fashioned nightgowns, she'd taught him an erotic lesson he'd never forget. He didn't need that kind of memory tonight. He had a more interesting plan in mind.

It would be, he hoped, the successful beginning of his courtship of the woman he still loved.

"Why are you hiding behind the door?" she asked, sniffing between every other word.

"Your sneezes are the things of which legends are made," he quipped, sliding around the edge so she could see him better. "But if you're finished?"

"For now." Kassidy sniffed again, looking over his shoulder into the dark house. "Does that mean I can come in?"

But Matt wasn't paying attention. He was peering toward the street, where she'd left her car. Spotlighted by the street lamp, her rather skewed parking job resembled the work of a drunk.

"What's your front tire doing on my lawn?"

"I sneezed."

"You know better than to drive when your allergies are kicking up," he said mildly, pulling her inside before closing the door, purposely ignoring the small, overnight bag that was sitting on the porch. "Especially that car. It's a menace."

"The car runs fine!" she protested. "It just needs a coat of wax."

"You've been saying that ever since I met you," he pointed out, throwing an arm around her shoulders as they strolled by silent agreement toward the kitchen.

"Yeah, well, I'll get around to it someday."

"Not in *that* car's lifetime," he countered, flipping on the kitchen light.

"Atchoo!"

"That's your answer for everything."

In the dark hallway, Kassidy failed to see the sneakers in her path and would have fallen, if his arm hadn't tightened around her as she stumbled. "I see you haven't changed your habits any," she said, sneezing both before and after the comment.

"If you're referring to my housekeeping skills . . ."

"Or lack of," she retorted.

"Whatever," he said with a shrug. "I guess being neat and tidy isn't one of my personal goals." Pushing her toward the high stools at the counter, Matt shoved a pile of old newspapers out of the way, so he could see her better, then moved to the refrigerator and pulled out the milk. "Hot chocolate, I presume?" he asked.

Kassidy just sniffed loudly and nodded her head. "Your mother should have hung a label around your neck— something like Beware. Slob on Premises."

"You're cruisin' pretty close to the wind for someone who wants some of my premium hot chocolate," he said in a falsely stern voice. Then he changed the subject, because he hadn't meant to let her walk into a messy house; he'd simply forgotten to straighten up and was mad at himself. "What was it this time?" he asked, stirring the milk in the pan. "Roses from your new boyfriend? Or did you forget that strawberries are not your best friends?"

"There's no boyfriend." Sneezing again, even louder than before, Kassidy grabbed the edge of the counter as her chair threatened to topple.

Matt shrugged. "How was I to know? It's been a while since I've seen you."

Three weeks, Kassidy thought silently. Three long, lonely weeks. But thoughts like that didn't get her anywhere, not these days. Their divorce was final. They'd accomplished the impossible—parting as friends—friends who still kept up with each other, more or less.

But it had been three weeks since she'd seen him at the restaurant with that athletic-looking blonde, who'd seemed to hang on his every word—not to mention quite a few parts of his body. Three weeks since Warren had taken her out for a candlelight dinner in an attempt to revive their mutually flagging interest.

The evening had not been the success either had hoped, although Kassidy was convinced her lack of response to Warren's efforts had been a direct result of Matt's presence across the room.

Perhaps she needed to give Warren another chance, she mused, watching Matt pour the chocolate into heavy mugs. Maybe she'd call him tomorrow and see if he'd be interested in trying again. Not that it would be a disaster if he said no, she admitted. Warren had been a friendly face in her office for so long that she really couldn't make up her mind if she preferred him as a friend or a date.

"I can't believe you made the old strawberry mistake," he said, plunking the mug in front of her. Looking at her, her eyes red from rubbing and her nose swollen from overuse, he remembered the time when he'd first encountered Kassidy's allergies. They'd been married no more than a week, and he'd gotten out of bed to make her a surprise breakfast—Belgian waffles with fresh strawberries. Kassidy hadn't wanted to spoil his surprise, he later found out, and had eaten the whole thing.

The hives had attacked within the hour, and he'd spent the morning rubbing calamine lotion onto the swollen welts. He'd always remember that morning, but not because he'd felt guilty. Rather, he remembered why she'd eaten the strawberries in the first place—because she loved him, she'd said. Then she'd told him she loved breakfast in bed, and to use blueberries next time, please.

Matt didn't take a chair, but leaned on the counter, cupping the mug of chocolate within his long, thick fingers. There had been many scenes like this, Kassidy found herself thinking, countless times when they'd talked until past midnight over hot chocolate. They never seemed to get enough of that. Talk, that was.

"Not strawberries," she finally said, dragging open the zipper of her coat as the chocolate began to warm her.

Matt snapped his fingers as though he'd just remembered something. "That's right. You get hives from strawberries, not the sneezes."

Kassidy nodded, sniffing once before she spoke again. "It wasn't strawberries. Cat."

"Your date brought you a cat?" The nightgown had pink and blue flowers on it, lots of them, clumped around some rather spectacular purple irises. He'd never seen this one before. It wasn't a sight one was likely to forget.

"I told you, Matt," she protested evenly. "There was no date." Kassidy blew noisily into her tissue, then stuffed it into a deep pocket and pulled out a fresh one.

"So how'd you get cornered by a cat?" He smiled at the image, knowing he'd played a dirty trick, but feeling totally unrepentant. It had worked, and that was all that mattered.

"My idiot roommate—" she almost snarled and took a deep drink of the chocolate "—rescued this mangy critter from a gutter somewhere and brought it home."

"So have her send it to a kennel or whatever," he suggested, as though there were no problem. "It's your condo. You make the rules."

"Marla called the kennel—shelter, I guess. It's closed until Monday. And she says if she can't at least keep the cat over the weekend, she'll move out."

"Had quite a battle, did you?"

"Not really," she confessed reluctantly. "The thing looked so wretched, I kind of had to feel sorry for it." Besides, roommates as accommodating as Marla were few and far between. The cat episode aside, the two women normally managed to coexist with a minimum of hassle.

"That must be a first. If I remember correctly, your reaction to cats is about the worst of any of the allergies."

"Right up there with strawberries," she sniffed in agreement, gulping down the rest of her chocolate. "I thought by staying in my room I'd get through the weekend, but no such luck."

"So what are you doing here?"

"There aren't many people I can just drop in on at one in the morning. I didn't think you'd mind." She held her breath, looking everywhere but at Matt.

"Did it occur to you I might be, er, busy?"

"Yes." Kassidy forced herself to look at him then, clenching her teeth to keep her chin from trembling. "It occurred to me. I figured if it wasn't convenient to answer the door bell, you wouldn't."

But he had, and never in her life had she felt such overwhelming relief.

"Which explains why you didn't just use your key," he said lightly, pleased she hadn't taken him for granted. Kassidy knew he had a personal life, just as he was aware she had recently begun dating. Admitting that there was nothing left to tie them together was important.

It was like starting from scratch. This time he wouldn't let the love overwhelm the details of living together. This time they needed to make it work *for*, not against them.

"I haven't used my key since I moved out," she said crossly. "I still don't know why you wanted me to keep it."

"Because the house is half yours," he said patiently, turning his back on her as he carried the empty mugs to the sink.

Kassidy raised her voice so he could hear her over the noise of the running water as he rinsed the cups. "You'll need the key back if you buy me out," she said. After the divorce they'd retained joint ownership of the house, partly because Matt hadn't made up his mind whether or not he wanted to stay there or sell, but mostly because Kassidy was reluctant to lose such a good investment. And since it was a *friendly* divorce, there hadn't seemed to be any rush to make a final decision.

They'd bought the house the week they married. Its furnishings were the result of a hilarious, two-day sweep through the major furniture stores in Seattle. Kassidy hated the idea of seeing their house go to strangers. But the other option, that of knowing Matt was living there among the things they'd chosen together, someday sharing their home with another woman—she hated that more.

"You need the money for something now?" he asked.

"It's appreciating just fine where it is," she said nonchalantly. "I'll let you know if I need my half."

"So until then, I guess you need to keep your key."

"Does that mean I can spend the night?"

"Of course not!" Matt chuckled at the sudden flush that colored her face a deep red. "Whatever gave you that idea?"

She gulped, surprised. This was even more difficult than she'd imagined. Begging a place to sleep from your ex-husband wasn't the choice she would have made if they hadn't remained such good friends.

Matt still helped out with the Scout troop that Kassidy co-led, providing equipment and guidance for their outings. In return, Kassidy had her Scouts bake cookies to raise money for the Little League and even took on the task of sewing the new team patches onto their uniforms.

With all that in common, it was a wonder she hadn't run into him during the past three weeks.

She tried begging. "You've got to let me stay, Matt! It's either you or Mom, and she's already overbooked."

"Your sister?" he asked, pretending he was guessing, but at the same time silently thanking Kassidy's mother, Amanda Canyon, for her cooperation.

Kassidy nodded, hope flickering again. "So how about it? You always said to come to you if I was in trouble."

"You're not in trouble, Kassidy," he chided. "You're just too cheap to go to a hotel for the night."

"*Three* nights!" she exclaimed. "That damned cat won't be out of there until Monday morning, and I'm not stepping a foot into that condo until its fumigated."

"So you're too cheap to go to a hotel for three nights," he amended, leaning back against the counter as he watched her marshal her arguments. He had an answer for every one of them—he'd prepared as he'd waited for the door bell to ring.

"I'm not too cheap—"

"Nonsense." Not much of an argument, but enough for his purpose. Besides, he didn't want to argue. There had already been enough of that.

She flushed again, remembering this had been one of the main conflicts that had torn them apart. Kassidy wasn't cheap, she'd always insisted. Just prudent. She didn't like throwing money away when alternatives—less costly alternatives—were available.

That's why she had an old car—transportation, she called it—that performed much better than it looked. While she paid proper attention to maintenance and safety, she totally ignored the more aesthetic points, like the peeling vinyl roof and the abundance of rust spots. It looked like a wreck, but drove, well, if not like a dream, at least she could claim it performed adequately. Matt, on the other hand, insisted on driving a flashy sports job that cost almost as much to maintain as it had to buy!

Kassidy didn't mind spending money on her career, not when it made the difference between success and stagnation. That was why her wreck of a car housed a telephone. It would have been more at home in Matt's car—unused, but much more at home.

With rare exceptions, the new clothes she bought were for work, where it was important to look good. Matt, on the other hand, spent a fortune on stuff he never wore out of the house, had even tried to buy drawerfuls of sexy underwear for her. Kassidy had never seen the sense in that, particularly when he'd always said he thought she'd look sexy in a sack. She'd shipped all the nonsense silks and satins back to the store, insisting on her perfectly suitable—and cheap and plain and serviceable—underwear.

Money, not the lack of it but how to spend it, had been a constant source of bickering, she recalled.

"I'm not too cheap to go to a hotel," Kassidy finally said, without admitting the thought had already crossed her mind. That would only prove his point. "I just thought the house was closer, and since we're such good friends, you wouldn't mind letting me use the guest room."

"I don't think so," he answered softly, not wanting to hurt her, but needing her to understand. "We're divorced and we just shouldn't do things like that—not if we're going to make this divorce work."

"You mean you don't trust yourself?" she joked, wondering what the hell he meant by "make this divorce work," but not having the nerve to ask.

"Perhaps I don't trust you," he shot back, wishing she hadn't skated over the divorce issue. It was too soon, he knew. She hadn't even begun to think yet, much less consider alternatives. "More important, I think the neighbors might get the wrong idea."

"You never cared about the neighbors before," she said evenly, realizing he was quite serious about not letting her stay. That possibility hadn't occurred to her, and she felt strangely bereft.

"We were married then. What we did was none of their business." He hesitated, wishing he'd prepared a stronger argument. What the neighbors thought hadn't mattered to him, still didn't. But for his purpose it was the only argument going, so he persisted. "I don't want to have to make explanations," he said. "With your car out front for the weekend, I'd have to give them one, and I'd rather not."

"So move the car."

"No, Kassidy." Pushing away from the counter, Matt went to the phone on the wall and punched the number for Information. Scribbling down the numbers of a nearby hotel and the local cab company, he started calling.

"I don't need a cab," she said crossly.

"Humor me. I'll pay for it." The hotel answered and put him on hold.

At first Kassidy let the remark go by; she'd lost the argument about being cheap once already. Then she tried again. "If I take a cab, the car will still be in front of the house," she stated triumphantly.

"So I'll drive it back to your condo first thing in the morning, before the neighbors are up," he said smoothly. "I can always run home from there. It's only a couple of miles."

"I thought you hated my car."

"I do. But I don't particularly like it on my front lawn, either."

Kassidy fumed a little, then realized she was close to pouting. She never pouted. Summoning her last resources, she made a final attempt. "I can drive."

"Not while you're still sneezing," he said, then ignored her as he made the arrangements with the hotel.

"I'm not sneezing anymore," she insisted, then was promptly bent double by the force of a gigantic explosion.

Matt called the cab company.

"'AND TOMMY SNUGGLED deep under his covers, his head full of the dreams that turn every little boy's life into a marvelous adventure. The End.'"

Kassidy closed her fingers over the book, watching the rapt expressions on the faces of the thirty-odd children gathered around her. Seated on a miniature chair, with the children on pillows or chairs or just sprawled on the carpet, she reveled in the enjoyment she shared with her young listeners. Story hour was always a special time in her week, more so now she knew all the boys and girls by name. Sandwiched between the intense hours she spent at the office on Saturdays, the spell with the children was a welcome respite.

"Can we have the story now about the little girl who followed her dog into the cave?"

Kassidy flashed a smile at the redheaded girl in the front row, whose braids and calico dress were reminiscent of another time. Michelle always asked for the same story, and Kassidy often imagined the child growing up with an enthusiasm for spelunking. Figuring it had to be at least three weeks since she'd read that particular book, she checked her watch, only to see there were just five minutes left.

"Okay, Michelle. But you have to bring it quickly. We're almost out of time." The book would take at least fifteen minutes to read, but Kassidy shrugged it off. The work she'd left on her desk would wait another quarter hour. And it wasn't as though there was anyone to complain. Most people in her office took their weekends seriously, filling them with recreation.

Kassidy took these hours seriously, as well. She used them to get ahead. With the exception of story hour, Little League games in the spring, and occasional Girl Scout projects, Saturdays might as well have been part of her regular working schedule.

Little Michelle dashed off to the shelves, slowing only as she passed in front of the librarian's desk. Running was not permitted, but childish enthusiasm was hard to squelch, and Michelle's was no exception. The moment she'd passed the desk, her little feet picked up the pace. The other children talked quietly among themselves as Kassidy watched Michelle disappear into the stacks that held the children's books.

"Hey, there's Coach!"

Bobby scrambled up from his place on the floor and dashed across the room to where Matt was looking through some magazines. Kassidy watched several other boys join him, seriously depleting the ranks of her group. But she didn't call them back. Instead she accepted the book from Michelle and opened it to the first page.

"Aren't you going to wait for the guys?" Pauline looked worried. Kassidy knew it was more because she had a crush on Bobby than because she didn't want them to miss anything.

"They'll be back," Kassidy said softly, "but our time is nearly up and we've got to keep going." She began the familiar story, ignoring the tingling at the back of her neck that signaled Matt's presence. He didn't even have to be near her to cause that reaction. Just having him in the same room would fan the flames of the slow fire deep inside her, the fire that never seemed to go out.

This time he was just a few feet away.

"Sorry to disrupt story hour," he murmured quietly from a place just behind her left shoulder. "I've told the boys it wasn't very polite of them to run off."

He startled her with his nearness. Usually she saw him coming, was prepared for the smell of him, the sound. This time he'd caught her unawares.

"I know why they run to you," she replied quietly, moving her head just enough to bring him into focus. *They adore you. How can anyone object to that?* "You're their hero," she said.

"They're just excited about the game, as usual," he said, the half grin on his face telling her the boys were not the only ones looking forward to it. Patting her shoulder as though to amplify his apology, he continued softly, "I should have remembered this was story hour. What with this and my Little League games every Saturday, we never did have a moment alone."

He was polite enough not to mention the hours she'd spent at the office, she noticed. Perhaps he didn't remember. It was hard to tell, particularly now as she felt the weight of his gaze on her lips and found herself remembering the heat of his mouth.

When he grinned, she knew he'd read her mind. Floundering under his amused stare, she blurted out the only response that came to mind. "We had Sundays." Sundays—the one and only guilt-free day of the week. That was then, of course. Now she worked most Sundays.

It was something she should have never said. Eyes closed, Kassidy cringed, wishing she could take back the words. But when she finally got up enough nerve to open her eyes again, Matt's gaze was directed at the children.

He hadn't heard, she guessed. Or perhaps she hadn't said it at all.

Relaxing, she realized it felt good, having Matt beside her. She wanted to prolong his visit, say something light and sophisticated and outrageous that would make him laugh when he thought of her. But with the children shifting restlessly in the background, it was impossible to think straight. At least, she blamed it on the children. Then Matt was gone, with a careless wave of his hand, before she could organize her thoughts.

Watching him make his way back into the stacks at the far end of the library, she remembered she hadn't thanked him for sending Marla down to the hotel with her car this morning so she wouldn't have to take another cab. His special blend of thoughtfulness shouldn't have surprised her. She'd missed that since the divorce.

Impatient with her impossible thoughts, Kassidy decided to call Warren and ask him to dinner at the hotel restaurant. Then she restarted the story of the little girl who followed her dog into a cave.

Ten minutes later Matt left, although Kassidy pretended not to notice. The only outward sign she gave was to stumble over the sentence she was reading.

And if there was disappointment in her voice, the children didn't seem to notice.

MATT PAUSED at the top of the library steps, breathing deeply as he remembered the look on her face when he'd mentioned their Saturday schedule. Seeing her fight to hold back the memories was gratifying. And encouraging.

He hadn't been at all sure of her when he formulated this plan. He still wasn't, but that look she'd worn had given him some much-needed hope.

Perhaps, just perhaps she missed him as much as he missed her.

Taking another breath of the pine-scented air, Matt made his way down the steps toward the bicycle he'd left leaning against a tree. It wouldn't do to have her come out and find him daydreaming, not if she, too, was still caught up in the memories he'd stirred.

Because this time, he didn't want her seduced by the good things—not the least of which was the incredible attraction they'd shared . . . and the love. Both of them had been overwhelmed, blind to the intricacies of maintaining an intimate liaison with a virtual stranger.

Matt pushed the bike along the sidewalk, taking his time as he remembered what Kassidy's mother had said about the mess they'd made of their marriage. Matt had gone over to renew their friendship one afternoon after the divorce had become final. When Amanda brought up the subject of the divorce, he'd been startled and intrigued. It wasn't like her to interfere, he'd thought. And besides, her timing was all off. It was too late.

"Did it ever occur to you that you and Kassidy just didn't try to stay married?" Amanda Canyon had asked, her expression questioning, not condemning.

"We did try," Matt had argued. "We tried so hard, all we did was fight. It wasn't so much a marriage as a battle."

"Whatever gave you the idea that married people don't fight?"

"You, for one," he protested. "And my own parents. I never heard a harsh word between them."

"And from that you decided people in love don't fight?" she chided gently.

Matt had been at a loss as to where Amanda was leading him. "Kassidy and I both grew up in households where the only fighting was between the kids. When we got married, all we did was fight. It made sense that we weren't meant to be married."

"Did it ever occur to you that your parents might have had their arguments in private?" Kassidy's mother had asked, then pressed on before he could answer. "Or perhaps that most of the arguments had long since passed, before you were aware enough to notice?" Smiling at the puzzled expression on Matt's face, she'd continued. "I know it was that way with Bill and me. We fought quite a bit in the beginning. We still do occasionally."

"Then all married couples fight like we did?" Matt asked, incredulous because he knew better—or thought he did.

"Not always, but with you and Kassidy it was inevitable. You are different enough that changes needed to be made, if you were going to live with each other in any sort of peace. In a marriage, you each have to decide what you can give up in order to stay together. That's what it's all about . . . compromise."

"And Kassidy and I didn't compromise," Matt said without pride.

"You didn't even try."

Matt climbed onto his bike, smiling to himself as he remembered Amanda's eager support of his plan . . . including her refinements. The cat had been a stroke of genius. Amanda's stroke of genius.

Leaning forward on the racing handlebars, he pedaled into the mainstream of Saturday's sluggish traffic and kept pace with a blue van advertising fresh salmon. His stomach rumbled, and he contemplated following the van until it stopped, but changed his mind as it turned left and shot up a steep hill. He could always get fresh salmon. The amazing array of seafood was half the fun of living on the Puget Sound. And Federal Way, the town where he lived just south of Seattle, boasted a variety of excellent markets and restaurants.

He cycled a few more blocks west, then turned off the main road toward the water. His home was just a block or so from the Sound, but then, most of the houses around were within spitting distance of the water. It was kind of hard to avoid.

Pulling into the driveway, he braked and walked the bike around the garage and into its own little shed. There was room for two bikes, but Kassidy had never been interested enough to pick one out. Not that she'd had the time, of course. Her six-day work weeks had curtailed her extracurricular activities.

There were a lot of things they'd discovered they didn't agree upon during their marriage, and biking had been the least of them. Slamming the door, Matt jumped the garden wall and skirted the pool on his way to the back door.

They'd married in a rush, and divorced at the same speed.

This time Matt was determined they'd both go into the relationship with their eyes wide open.

He had to remember that, to keep in mind the problems that had seemed insurmountable twelve months ago. They were still there, still unsolved.

Unsolved, not unsolvable.

2

"YOU KNOW there's nowhere I'd rather be than with you, Kassidy...."

"Why, thank you, Warren."

"But don't you think we've watched enough of this?" he asked, referring to the Little League game she'd coerced him into attending.

"It's not over yet." Not for the first time since they arrived, Kassidy questioned the impulse that had made her invite Warren.

"How can you tell?"

"You mean, besides the scoreboard?"

"What scoreboard?"

"Over there." Kassidy pointed across the field. "Next to the refreshment stand, where Petey Allen is hanging up a zebra under the eighth inning."

"I thought that was a community graffiti project."

Kassidy shook her head vigorously. "The kids decided hanging numbers was too simple, so they enlarged the board to accommodate a little artistic freedom." She neglected to tell Warren about the perfectly legitimate scoreboard above the bleachers, just twenty feet or so behind them. If he'd been at all interested in the game, she figured he would have asked sooner.

"So what does the zebra have to do with baseball?"

"A zebra stands for zero," she explained patiently, her eyes following the kid sprinting for second. She let out an undignified whoop when he slid in under the mitt of the scrambling base man, then returned her attention to her date.

"It's really a very simple system," she said. "This way, the kids who aren't playing have something to do besides heckle their friends and eat hot dogs."

"Simple to you, maybe," Warren huffed, eyes narrowed on the colorful board across the field. "But you might tell me how to count the giraffe and two monkeys under the fifth inning."

"Three, of course. It's merely the number of objects in the square, Warren. Added up," she teased, trying to jolly him out of his somber mood. "Surely you can add?"

"Of course I can add." To prove it, he studied the board, using his fingers when he thought Kassidy wasn't looking. "As far as I can tell, the blue team is winning ten to eight."

"Uh-uh. Nine to eight." Kassidy shook her head without looking at him, crossing the fingers on one hand as Bobby stepped up to bat. Bobby had a problem with batting, Matt had told her. It was something they were working on, and Kassidy knew how important it was for the youngster to show his friends he could hit the ball at least once.

So far he'd never made it off home plate. And for extra pressure, they were already down two outs.

"What do you mean, 'Uh-uh'?" Warren rechecked his numbers. "It's ten to eight. I count three giraffes, two monkeys, a bear—"

"Not a bear," she corrected. "A sloth." Frowning, she watched as the first ball slipped past Bobby.

"Strike!" shouted the umpire. The crowd mumbled, shifting in their seats as they waited for the next pitch.

For an ordinarily calm man, Warren sounded as though he was getting a little excited. "Three giraffes, two monkeys, a *sloth*, three parrots and a leopard." Openly using his fingers now, he added them up. "That's ten."

"The leopard doesn't count."

"Why not?"

"It's the team mascot for the other side, the ones in yellow. Since the Blue Martians didn't make any runs that inning, someone from the Leopards snuck in their mascot in place of a zebra."

Another strike, and the half of the bleachers that supported the Blue Martians shouted their disagreement with the umpire's call. Kassidy automatically added her own two cents, her heart lurching as Matt left the dugout and headed across the field toward Bobby. She watched as the sun caught the lighter blond strands in his hair, knew how light they would become before the end of the season.

He walked easily, covering the ground with long strides. Kassidy's gaze swept over his long body, remembering how much pleasure she'd taken in watching him when they were married. Now, of course, she tried not to get caught at it.

She didn't think he'd mind if he knew.

"So you count everything except zebras and leopards,'" Warren persisted, all pretense of watching the game eclipsed by his determination to understand the scoring.

"More or less," she replied, her attention centered on the man and boy at home plate. She watched Matt as he grinned at the youth, hunkering down until they were at eye level. Bobby shuffled his feet as he listened to his coach, drawing patterns in the dirt with the wooden bat.

Kassidy felt her heart warm to the slowly growing smile on the boy's face. Two strikes, and any other coach would be sending in a pinch hitter. Not Matt.

Matt was telling a joke. She was sure of it, just as she knew Bobby would be allowed to finish his turn at bat.

Childish laughter mixed with a masculine chuckle. She watched as Matt playfully yanked Bobby's cap over his eyes before swinging into a lazy jog back to the dugout.

The game resumed.

"What do you mean, more or less?" Warren demanded, returning to his preoccupation with the scoreboard.

Kassidy ignored him as Bobby dug his feet into the dirt, raising his bat as the pitcher began his windup. The crowd, after a few shouts of encouragement, fell silent.

Kassidy crossed the fingers on her left hand. A few rows down, she noticed Pauline—the little girl from story hour with the crush on Bobby—with both sets of fingers crossed and eyes wide open behind the crossed wrists she held in front of her face.

"Kassidy—"

"Hush, Warren." She spoke firmly, paying scant attention to her date's indignation. It didn't matter, not when Bobby needed her support.

The crack of the ball against the bat brought the entire crowd to its feet, yellow and blue alike. They shouted and yelled and screamed directions as Bobby hustled off home plate.

Even when the first base man put him out, the shouting didn't stop.

It wasn't important that Bobby had made an out. Not today. It only mattered that he'd finally hit the ball.

"What's the big deal?"

"Sorry?" Kassidy sat down, the uproar gradually dying away as the teams exchanged places for the final inning. She watched as Bobby sprinted over to third base, exchanging high fives with a couple of teammates on his way. Now she could relax and enjoy the game. While Bobby might not be an ace batter, he played a mean third base.

"So the kid got a hit," Warren said. "Why all the hoopla?"

Kassidy sighed, trying to remind herself that this had been her idea, and Warren wasn't to blame. She'd honestly hoped he might enjoy the game, but Warren apparently wasn't the type of man who relished spending an afternoon watching Little League baseball. If she hadn't been so determined to show up with a date, Kassidy wouldn't have asked him at all.

It had never occurred to her to give the game a miss altogether, she realized abruptly.

"Nothing you'd find interesting," she said with more patience than she felt. "I guess you'd have to come every week to understand little triumphs like that."

"You come every week?" His tone was incredulous, his handsome face a picture of horror. "Ugh!"

"I try," she said, cringing at the white lie. She'd deliberately avoided the last two games, telling herself she had better things to do with her Saturdays—like work. And that way, if Matt encouraged the Amazonian blonde from the restaurant to attend the game, Kassidy wouldn't have to be nice to her.

Not that she minded that Matt was dating, she told herself. It was just a matter of his taste in women. Kassidy *knew* she didn't like the blonde, even without the benefit of meeting her.

But today she needed to be here. Bringing Warren along was a way to salve her pride. After last night, after her mistaken assumption that Matt would welcome her into what had once been their home, Kassidy needed to show him there were other men she could turn to.

"I guess I never figured you as a baseball fan," Warren said, sighing as he checked his watch.

"Not baseball," she murmured, eyes on the field. "Just Little League. It's more like a community event than a sport."

"It's still baseball," he grumbled, dropping his elbows to his knees as he prepared to wait out the last inning.

Kassidy glanced at his morose countenance, wondering how such a fit man could dislike one of America's favorite sports. To look at him, Warren was in terrific shape, a handsome man with a fabulous body. But then, perhaps he maintained his physique without the distraction of team sports. She shrugged, not particularly interested enough to ask. Warren was a friend—not a close one, but a friend, nevertheless. If he preferred sweating in front of a home video to stay in shape, she figured it was none of her business.

The Leopards were quickly trounced, yielding the game to the Blue Martians by the narrow margin of a single point.

"Now can we go?"

Kassidy dragged her attention from the victorious mob scene below with a final glance at Matt to confirm he didn't even know she was there. If he had known, there would have been a wave or a grin—an affirmation of the friendship they'd sworn to maintain. She frowned a little, wondering why he hadn't even bothered to look into the stands.

Sitting through the game with Warren had been a waste of time—Matt hadn't even noticed.

"Kassidy!"

Warren's irritable appeal tugged at her nerves, making her wonder if he'd been as bored as he acted. "Yes, Warren?" Trying very hard to remember Warren was a friend as well as a date, Kassidy attempted to smile.

"I asked if we could go home now."

"Go home?" With him? Kassidy shook her head in an attempt to clear the fog from her thought processes. "We can't go home, Warren," she explained patiently with a playful grin. "We don't have that kind of relationship."

"You always take everything I say so literally!" But he grinned back at her, seeming delighted to have her attention once again. "I was simply proposing—"

"Don't say that word unless you mean it!" she teased, laughing at the momentary shock in his eyes.

"If I didn't know you better, I'd say you were flirting with me," he said, shooting her a calculating look that lightened when he saw the amusement in her expression. Chagrined that he'd fallen for such an obvious joke, he groaned, standing to brush the dust from his trousers. Then he reached down to pull Kassidy to her feet, brushing at the patches of dust on her slacks as though he were tending a child.

"Whatever gave you the idea I wasn't flirting?" she asked, following him down the bleachers and across the dirt lot to his foreign compact. "I'd hate to think you only went out with me because you didn't want to hurt my feelings." Not that the few evenings they'd spent together had been unforgettable moments in time, she admitted. But it kind of hurt her pride that his interest was so . . . lacking!

"That's only why I came to the game," he admitted, dropping into the driver's seat before reaching across to unlatch her door. "I go out to dinner with you because you're good company and I love eating out."

"If all you want is a warm body so you can order Chateaubriand for two, why don't you ask Millie from across the hall?" she asked, referring to a woman she knew who was employed by the legal firm across the hall from the brokerage where they worked. Millie had also convinced Kassidy to help out with her Girl Scout troop. That had been nearly two years ago, and although it had taken a lot of convincing on Millie's part, Kassidy now wouldn't give up her spot as Co-Troop Leader for anything. She loved working with the group of preteen girls, even though sometimes it was quite a race to fit Scout meetings into her busy schedule.

Still, Kassidy thought, as she watched as Warren pushed the key into the ignition, she wasn't particularly in the mood to experience yet another rejection. After the disaster of her divorce, her ego certainly wasn't ready for Warren's almost embarrassing lack of interest. Knowing her own interest was lukewarm didn't lessen the minor blow, either.

Things didn't get any better.

"I *have* asked her, several times. She won't."

"Won't what?" Kassidy curled up on the tiny, velour-covered seat, her own self-indulgent sulks put aside as her interest was caught by Warren's rueful admission.

"Won't even let me walk her to the elevator," he muttered, swinging the tiny car toward an even tinier gap in the traffic. "She claims her conscience won't allow her to be seen with a man of my reputation."

Kassidy smothered a giggle, knowing exactly what gossip said about Warren. Looking at him, with his striking black hair and the sculpted lines of his face, tanned by a recent visit to Hawaii, not to mention the blue-gray eyes that easily seduced any woman who looked his way, Kassidy found herself almost wishing the gossip were true.

It wasn't, though. Warren was a very considerate and polite date, even a bit boring if he got onto the subject of market swings and trends. Kassidy had worked with him for years, and had never once seen any proof of the rumors of his Casanova alter ego.

"Have you tried explaining to her that nonsense is nothing more than a vicious rumor?"

"Not likely!" He laughed then, turning into the driveway of the hotel. "That 'nonsense,' as you call it, has been circulating for so long, it no longer has rumor status. Even the guys back in sales have been hitting me up for pointers about the various women in the office."

"What do you say to them?"

"I just tell them a gentleman never shares his secrets, nor the secrets of the women he's known." Then, pretending he didn't notice her uncontrolled laughter, he leaned across to push open the door. "I'll be back in an hour," he said sternly.

Kassidy saw a bright red flush adorn his cheeks as he pulled away.

MATT REACHED for the pitcher of root beer, pouring another round into all the plastic glasses within reach before topping off his own. The noise level in the pizza parlor was no worse than normal, although the exuberance of the triumphant Blue Martians seemed to drive the general pandemonium to new heights. Another enthusiastic toast to Bobby drove the volume even higher, and Matt was relieved when the pizza finally arrived to distract the boys.

"I still don't see why we couldn't have real beer." Muttering just loud enough for Matt to hear, Charlie eyed the brown liquid as though it were an evil substance. "It's not like the kids don't know we do stuff like that once in awhile."

"Do we have to have this same argument every week?" Matt grinned at the team manager, who was seated on the bench beside him. "You know how I feel about associating drinking with sports."

Charlie frowned as he reached forward to pull a large slice of pizza onto his plate, and Matt chuckled when Petey snatched the platter out of the manager's reach. Throwing Petey an evil stare, Charlie stood up and dragged another platter from the far end of the table.

"I'm not saying we let the kids drink," Charlie argued, eager to win the battle for a change. "They probably wouldn't like it, anyway."

Looking around at the assortment of nine-, ten- and eleven-year-olds, Matt knew that although these kids were young enough to prefer soft drinks, they were still impressionable. Matt felt that the adults had a responsibility to set an example.

"I'll bet that if we ordered dark beer for us, they wouldn't know the difference."

"I would."

Charlie muttered something Matt couldn't hear, then grabbed the evil stuff and chugged it. Still grinning, Matt poured him another glass without batting an eye. "I think you're a fraud, Charlie. You consistently manage to drink more root beer than the rest of us put together."

"I'm just a thirsty man, Matt. But I do wish we'd get the diet stuff next time. All that sugar is going to my belly!" Patting the conspicuous roll around his stomach with one hand, Charlie reached for some more pizza.

"Don't blame the root beer, Charlie. You've been carrying around that spare tire for longer than I can remember, and I know you weren't drinking root beer before you started managing the team."

Charlie appeared to ignore the jibe, concentrating instead on the pizza. With the rest of the team equally intent on filling their stomachs, Matt hoped his own meager efforts would pass unnoticed. The single slice of pizza he'd taken earlier was still on his plate, untouched and congealing. Wishing he'd eaten the spicy concoction when it was hot, Matt forced himself to take a bite.

It was revolting—precisely as he'd expected. But he chewed as fast as was safe, then took another bite. And another.

A few moments later it was over.

Matt kept the smile plastered on his face, feigning a full stomach when Charlie shoved another piece in his direction. "No can do, buddy," he protested. "I've had my share."

Charlie shrugged, pulling the slice onto his own plate. "Doesn't seem natural, your not liking pizza." Opening his mouth over the wedge laden with pepperoni, anchovies and olives, Charlie took an enormous bite.

"Don't talk so loud," Matt cautioned, checking the faces around the table for anyone paying attention. "I don't want the kids to know."

"Afraid they'll think you're less than perfect?"

Matt shook his head, wondering how much longer he could keep the secret from the boys. "This is their favorite place," he murmured. "If they found out how much I detest pizza, they'd get all polite and suggest somewhere else."

"I think you overestimate the boys," Charlie said, washing down the pizza with more root beer. "Courtesy rarely interferes with their appetites."

"I guess you'd know." Matt laughed and easily deflected the halfhearted punch Charlie threw at him.

Charlie wrapped his fingers around another slice and nibbled at a loose sausage before asking, "So who was the toy boy sitting with Kassidy?"

Matt stiffened, surprised only that Charlie hadn't brought up the subject before. The team manager had been vocal in his disapproval of Matt's divorce, and the intervening year hadn't lessened his criticism. Ignoring his question wouldn't accomplish anything, mostly because Charlie had the persistence of a terrier—he'd keep asking until he got an answer!

Matt cleared his throat. "I'm told he has a mind of his own, a rather sharp one, in fact."

"No wonder you were so distracted." Charlie reached for the root beer pitcher and refilled his glass. "It's one thing watching her go around with a gorgeous guy, but a guy with brains! Well, it's no wonder she divorced you."

"You telling me I'm not pretty enough?" Matt demanded.

Charlie snickered and elbowed Matt hard in the ribs. "Naw. You're just stupid. Any man with brains wouldn't have let her go."

Matt sighed and shook his head. With Charlie, it was a no-win situation. Inevitably he managed to bring the subject around to Kassidy. And just as inevitably, he pointed out what an idiot Matt had been in agreeing to the divorce. Ignoring the satisfied grin on the other man's face, Matt sipped his root beer as his thoughts left the pizza parlor and slipped back to the game. The end of the game, actually, when he'd watched Kassidy drive off with Warren.

His brows came together as he thought about that, trying to make sense out of their presence at the game. He'd heard about Warren's reputation, just as he'd listened to Kassidy's assurances that the notoriety was totally false. She'd shared all the office gossip with him while they were married. She'd insisted those rumors about Warren were undeserved.

So maybe Warren had grown into his notoriety over the last year. The glimpse Matt had gotten of Warren stroking his hands all over her body had nearly sent him bounding up the bleachers. But he hadn't done it, mostly because the stroking had stopped before he could get himself untangled from the mayhem on the field.

By that time they'd been heading for the parking lot without a backward glance. Even though he'd purposely avoided staring at them all afternoon, he was indignant when they left without a word.

He hadn't made the effort to say hello because he was afraid the jealousy he was feeling would sneak out and betray him. Letting Kassidy know how he felt wasn't appropriate—not yet. First she needed to discover her own feelings for him—if there were any.

Matt gripped his plastic glass a little harder. He'd known she had dated Warren a few times, just as she'd seen a couple of other men.

But he hadn't taken it seriously. Clenching the empty fist of his other hand, Matt wondered if he'd made a strategic error. Perhaps Kassidy didn't miss him at all.

Perhaps, just perhaps, she was enjoying her freedom.

A knife-edged pain shot through his chest as he considered the possibility. The image of Kassidy with another man hurt unbearably. The only cure that would help would be holding Kassidy in his arms again. He knew that, just as he knew he'd never stop trying. Shutting his eyes against the pain, Matt deliberately pushed away the debilitating doubt.

Lifting his eyes to stare blankly across the room, Matt focused on the night before, when she'd come to him. True, she'd been running from a dreaded cat. Also true, she'd been attempting to avoid a costly excursion.

But she'd come to him. Not to Warren, not to any other man.

Holding that thought, he made plans to see her again. Tonight, he decided. Even if she was still with Warren, *especially* if she was with Warren, Matt knew he needed to see her tonight.

By striking when she least expected, he hoped to rattle her complacent acceptance of their divorce.

"I THOUGHT you'd be out with the team."

Her eyes darted toward the door of the lounge, wondering if he'd brought the team here to the hotel. When she didn't see a single youthful face grinning back at her, she remembered the time. It was too late for the kids to be out.

But that didn't answer the question of why Matt was here, at the hotel to which he'd banished her last night!

"And I thought you'd be out with Warren."

"I am—I was," she said as Matt stared pointedly at the empty chair beside her. "He just left," she protested as an eyebrow quirked in disbelief. Angry that she'd allowed herself to become perturbed by Matt's sudden appearance, Kassidy went onto the offensive. "And since when is keeping up on my social life a part of the divorce agreement?"

"Have a fight?" he asked, ignoring the question. Matt, too, had been surprised to see Warren walk out just a few moments earlier. At the very least, he'd been expecting to crash their date and make it a threesome.

"It's late. He just needed to get home," she said evenly, wishing she'd not elected to remain in the hotel's lounge after Warren had departed. But the piano music had calmed her, the Cole Porter tunes soothing her emotions, lessening her depression.

Why she was depressed, she couldn't have said. Warren's confessed attraction to Millie certainly didn't have anything to do with it, although it had been rather galling to spend an entire meal listening to her date bemoan his frustrated courtship of another woman.

Even her enforced stay at the hotel had nothing to do with her mood. While the condo was full of nasty cat germs, her room here was wonderfully sterile.

And she'd convinced herself that Matt's refusal to take her in was simply a minor irritation.

"Good thing I came along, then," he said, signaling the waitress. "I'd hate to think you were lonely."

"I'm not lonely," she insisted. "What are you doing here, anyway?" It didn't make sense, not after he'd ignored her at the game. She was definitely miffed about that, and just as determined not to let him know.

Matt ignored her question as the cocktail waitress strolled over to the table and took Matt's order for a club soda for himself and wine for Kassidy before she could protest. "I don't want another glass of wine," she said to the waitress's back, not surprised when her refusal received no attention.

"So don't drink it," he suggested, his gaze drifting lazily around the bar. "I just thought if you were staying . . ."

Kassidy bit her tongue. It was no use fighting with Matt when he wasn't in the mood for confrontation. She swerved back to a variation on her original question. "How did you know I'd be here?"

"I didn't," he said truthfully. If she'd been out, he would have waited. If she'd been in her room, he would have made up some pretense for visiting her there. It was merely a stroke of luck that she was in the lounge.

Kassidy sighed heavily and closed her eyes. Trying to get information out of Matt was frustrating. It was something she'd never mastered. Instead it had always been a matter of finally stumbling over the right question before she learned anything at all.

The right question. Kassidy concentrated on reducing the situation to its basics, seeking a possible approach.

"Did you come here to see me, Matt?"

He grinned, delighted she'd remembered how to play. "I'm always happy to see you, Kassidy," he said softly. "You know that."

Conscious that she was getting close to the answer she sought, Kassidy ignored the warmth of his response and persisted. "That's not what I asked. I want to know if you came to see me."

He shook his head, the lie that wasn't really a lie taking some of the joy out of his mood. "I'm here to see Jack. He promised to help back the lacrosse tournament next month, and we need to get the details ironed out." Just because that could have been done anytime at all didn't mean he couldn't do it tonight, Matt assured himself. It wasn't really a lie—not a big one, anyway.

Disappointed, Kassidy pretended curiosity. "Who's Jack?"

"The manager." Digging into his pocket, Matt handed the waitress cash in payment for the drinks. He didn't look at Kassidy, not after that fleeting look of disappointment he'd seen. He began telling her about the game that afternoon.

"But I was there!"

Kassidy was amazed by the disbelief on his face. Surely he'd seen her, hadn't he? The field wasn't that big, the number of spectators wasn't that large. But perhaps this explained why he hadn't waved.

"I thought you worked most Saturdays."

"I try to make the games," she pointed out, a little piqued he didn't remember. "Even when we were married, I tried."

"That's right!" he exclaimed as if suddenly remembering. "I guess I forgot." Then he grinned as though pleased she'd bothered to come, totally skipping over the hint that he hadn't noticed. "Didn't Bobby do a fine job!" he enthused, then went on to tell her the joke he'd shared with the young boy.

Kassidy watched his face, felt herself being drawn into his enthusiasm. The joy they shared in working with children had always been like this. Whether they talked about her Scouts or his team, it was as though they spoke of family.

The ability he had to understand how she felt about the children was one of the things she missed. It wasn't something he'd had to work at, because he felt the same. The children had been the one thing they had in common. That was why they'd imagined a marriage between them would work, because of the children . . . and their common goal to have a family.

But she knew that two people who couldn't live together in a semblance of harmony didn't have the right to bring children into the world. Kassidy and Matt had discovered that their basic incompatibility in everything else made everyday living a test of wills.

There'd been no attempt to compromise, not even a suggestion that there was a halfway point. Kassidy had simply stolen time from work to be with Matt, forgetting her ambition whenever he called.

They'd played hooky together, hiding in darkened movie theaters like misbehaving adolescents, watching the latest sci-fi films and throwing popcorn at the bad guys on the screen. Or they'd borrowed a catamaran and skimmed over the waters of the Puget Sound until the sun fell behind the hills and it was too cold to sail anymore.

He'd always been there, ready to share another adventure with her, an hour or two stolen from reality, *her* reality. The rugged backpacking trips of which he'd talked had never taken place, mostly because he hadn't wanted to leave her for even a few days, and she'd refused to go along.

It had been all or nothing, and it hadn't worked.

"Kassidy?"

She stared at him, heard him call her name. But it was hard, remembering where they were now . . . and where they'd been.

"Did I bore you to death?" he asked softly, watching as the last of a myriad emotions slipped across her face.

"Never," she said emphatically, forgetting for a moment that there were feelings she shouldn't divulge to Matt. It wasn't productive to tell him that she vividly remembered every moment they'd shared . . . or that she was having trouble letting each one go. "I guess I was just remembering . . ."

"The game?" he prodded, his voice low and husky and a little amused, as though he could read her thoughts.

"Not really," she said softly, lifting her eyes to his steady gaze. There was a lump in her throat that impeded her breathing, and her vision seemed to blur as she held Matt's gaze. "It all seems so long ago.... But listening to you talk about Bobby brings it back."

"Brings what back, Kassidy?" Matt held his breath, surprised that she was prepared to talk about their relationship. That was something they'd avoided since the divorce. They just went on, friends pretending they'd never been anything else.

He smiled, insinuating himself into her mood and her mind, his gaze fastened on the mouth he longed to kiss. But he waited, giving her the chance to make the first move.

"The good times," she breathed, conscious that he was leaning closer, his eyes on her lips, which were suddenly dry. And then, just because she wanted to know—*had* to know—she touched the tip of her tongue to the corner of her mouth, watched as his hungry gaze followed the wet trail across her lips.

He wanted her! Kassidy fought the unevenness of her breathing, almost light-headed at her discovery. She waited, faintly aware of an emotion that resembled relief coursing through her veins.

His eyes were burning with unmasked arousal as he leaned into her, just a breath away from her parted lips. Kassidy wondered for a moment if he could see her own excitement, then gave up thinking as she savored the anticipation of his kiss. "This is not something we should do," he murmured against her lips, brushing their softness with deliberate restraint.

Kassidy shuddered, her hands gripping the chair as she gave herself up to the soft caress of his mouth. She wanted to reach out and pull him against her, to satisfy the longing to hold him . . . and be held. She'd missed him so damned much! His lips brushed hers again, lightly, and she opened her mouth to him.

"Don't do that, Kassidy," he groaned, resisting the invitation.

Dumping her pride in one fell swoop, she begged. "Please!"

"Sorry, honey," he breathed into her mouth. "We can't." But he took his time about retreating, touching her mouth one last time with his own, his lips barely resting against hers. Being this close again was a piece of heaven. And hell.

With a sigh that expressed his frustration, Matt leaned back into his chair, stretching his legs under the table in an effort to ease the pressure against the seams of his trousers. Her response had almost been his undoing, her deliberate enticement an exciting surprise.

But sex wasn't enough.

"Sorry about that, honey," he said, grinning lopsidedly. "You always did manage to get me aroused faster than any woman I've ever known."

"I wasn't trying—" she protested before he cut in.

"The hell you weren't!" He laughed, the sound short and disbelieving. "I'm the man you married, remember? I *know* when you want my mouth on yours." She colored, astonished that he could talk so casually about such an intimate subject.

"No sense in blushing, Kassidy. It was only a kiss."

"Not even much of one at that," she chided, deciding that if he could talk about it, then so could she. "You used to do better."

His grin widened. "When we were married, I could afford to get carried away."

Kassidy sighed heavily, admitting defeat. There was no way she could hold her own in this dialogue. She faked a yawn to avoid having to respond.

"Tired?" he asked softly as he correctly interpreted the evasion. Matt flicked a glance at his watch, waiting for the fib that was sure to come.

"Guess so," she said, yawning again as added proof. "It's been a long day." A *very* long day, she told herself, that had begun sometime last night.

"Don't let me keep you, then. I should probably go hunt up Jack before he forgets I'm here." Not giving her a chance to protest, Matt shifted to his feet and held out a hand to Kassidy. "Come on, I'll walk you to the elevator."

"I'm pretty sure I can find it myself," she said, although she slipped her hand into his without a second thought. "I don't want to keep you from your meeting."

"No bother." He grinned, keeping her soft hand in his as they strolled across the lobby. "Jack's office is next to the elevators."

And that, she mused, told her where she stood. Tugging her hand away from the warmth, Kassidy marched independently to the elevator. She reached ahead to punch the button and was relieved to have the door slide open at her command.

She stepped inside before she could change her mind. "Thanks for the wine, Matt." Jamming her finger onto the control panel, she kept a smile plastered on her face as she waited for the doors to close.

"See you around, Kassidy."

See you around. The doors shut between them, leaving Kassidy to wonder why that sounded like a promise.

3

"I SWEAR I saw less of you when we were married!"

Kassidy shook her head in disbelief. There he was again, where she least expected him . . . when she least expected. Running into him again was against all the odds. In the week since she'd left the hotel she'd seen him everywhere.

Matt looked down at his cutoff jeans and sweatshirt before gazing wickedly at Kassidy. "You're right. I seem to remember showing you *a lot* more than naked knees, honey," he said, seeing his words bring a hot blush to her face.

"That's not what I meant!" she sputtered, then deliberately pushed the shopping cart over his toes. Ignoring his modified bellow of protest, she rolled the cart down the aisle toward the frozen dinners. "I meant I can't seem to go anywhere without running into you!"

"Over me is more like it!" he grumbled, wincing as much at the boxes she was chucking into the cart as at his sore toes.

"That's your own fault," she pointed out. "Just like yesterday, when I was washing my car. You wouldn't have gotten drenched if you hadn't ridden your bike in front of the hose."

"I wasn't in front of the hose until you turned it on me," he shot back, grinning at her confusion.

"Well, you surprised me, zooming up like that with no warning," Kassidy complained. "Seems like every time I turn around, you're there."

"I'm not always around," he protested. "You just haven't been noticing me until lately. Any special reason?" He picked up one of the boxes from her basket and read the ingredients, swallowing the wave of near nausea that provoked, and shaking his head in disgust. The things she insisted upon putting into her stomach! His eyes traveled to where her tummy peeked out from between her cropped top and shorts, and he was once again amazed at the lack of outward signs of her abominable diet.

"Not noticing!" she exclaimed, grabbing the box before he could return it to the shelf. Conscious that Matt was directing his bewildered gaze to the vicinity of her belly, she gave her shirt a futile tug. "A day hasn't passed this week that I haven't seen you at least twice."

"You're counting?"

Kassidy fumed, wishing she knew what he was about. Ever since she'd returned home from the hotel—thanks to a cat-loving friend of Marla's, who'd offered to take the scrawny thing out of the condo and into her own home—Matt had been everywhere she'd looked.

On Monday he'd sauntered into the bakery just as she was paying for her doughnuts. She'd waited by the door, wondering what she could possibly say to him that would sound casually indifferent as she ostensibly looked for her car keys. But he'd only winked a friendly good-morning before shoving a bran muffin into his mouth and sauntering across the road toward the park.

That night he'd been at the Friends of the Library meeting, seated across the room next to Bobby's mother. He'd waved, and she thought it would be a nice touch of indifference if she avoided saying hello during the coffee hour that followed. After all, she didn't want him to think he had to speak to her every time they met. But Matt hadn't stayed for coffee and had slipped out without a word.

Kassidy seethed; she hated being upstaged.

On Tuesday he and Charlie had met for lunch at the same restaurant where Kassidy was eating with a client. She'd ignored him.

Later that evening, as she'd waited in her car at the fast-food restaurant's drive-thru window, she'd been startled to see Matt cycling past. Twice. By the time the sack with its double cheeseburger and onion rings was on the seat beside her, he'd disappeared.

And so on. And so on.

"I'm not counting," she fibbed, and tossed three packages of potato chips on top of the frozen dinners. "It just seems you're around more than before."

"It's your imagination," he said, nimbly substituting cholesterol-free chips for the ones she'd taken. "I suppose when I show up at the charity dinner next week, you'll think I followed you."

"You're not going to the dinner!" So surprised was she by his announcement that she let the chip exchange go uncorrected. "You *never* go to those things!"

"Times change, sweetheart," he murmured, urging her toward the fresh-vegetable aisle where he began to fill his own basket. "And I've been told I look rather distinguished in evening clothes." Snagging a bag of spinach, he dropped it into her cart.

"Don't lie to me, Matt Hill!" Kassidy warned, tossing the spinach back onto the shelf. "The only time you've ever worn a tux was when you were ring bearer at your aunt's wedding, thirty years ago!"

"And I looked terrific," he said smoothly, enjoying the way her eyes flashed in frustrated disbelief. He wanted to kiss her then, take her face between his hands and hold her still for his mouth. A real kiss this time, hot and wet and wild. And this time, he wouldn't retreat.

He could imagine how it would begin, his fingers threading into the glossy mass of curls as his lips smoothed across hers. She would open her mouth to him, stroke his tongue with the tip of hers as she welcomed him to the moist warmth. And when he was all the way inside, with his tongue stroking deep and hard, her fingers would rise to clutch at his shoulders as she gave up a sweet moan into his mouth.

"Matt, will you stop!"

"Stop what?" He cleared his throat, focusing his attention on the here and now with great difficulty.

"Stop putting all that junk in my cart," she scolded, plucking out the bunches of radishes and celery stalks, which were crushing the potato chips. "You know I won't eat any of that stuff!"

"Your diet is disgusting." Reaching across her to an upper shelf in the refrigerated unit, he selected three containers of tofu and added them to the vegetables in his basket.

Seeing the tofu, Kassidy raised a curved eyebrow. "Disgust is in the eyes of the beholder," she said. "I don't think I can take anymore of this tonight. If I have to watch you pick out wheat germ, I think I'll throw up. Good night, Matt."

He grinned, counting this skirmish as a victory of sorts. After all, Kassidy was taking home the cholesterol-free chips.

And she'd admitted that she'd noticed him. That was important, Matt knew. Not just because she'd been aware of him, but because she'd actually said something about it.

Matt took a deep breath and purposely turned toward the back of the store. It was time for part two of his plan, and now was as good a time to begin as any.

Now that Kassidy had admitted to being aware of him, it was time to disappear.

KASSIDY LOOKED AT HERSELF in the cheval glass that stood beside the dresser and wondered if Matt would notice the difference. *Of course he won't notice,* she chided herself. The change was on the inside, invisible under the strapless, teal-blue gown, with its impossibly tight bodice and flowing skirt.

Not that it was metaphysical or anything like that, Kassidy argued. But perhaps Matt would think so, drawing an analogy between her new underwear and some internal attitude change.

Lingerie, she corrected herself. She'd always bought underwear before. Tonight, for the first time, she was wearing lingerie. Frivolous, sensuous lingerie—just like the bits of silky nonsense Matt had tried to give her long ago.

Not that there was much of it, just panties and silky nylons. And the lacy garter belt, she remembered, wondering why she'd never tried one before. It was a marvelous sensation—positively erotic—these little bits of silk and lace, a creamy-white contrast to her slightly darker flesh.

No, Matt wouldn't notice. A pity, Kassidy lamented. He'd be the only man there tonight who might appreciate the whim that had produced such surprising results.

If he was there tonight.

Her brow puckered as she tried to imagine where he'd been all week. It had been a startling change of pace—almost unbalancing. Just when she had gotten to the point of noticing him practically every time she looked up, he'd disappeared. Completely.

Kassidy chewed on her lip, frustrated with the week-long sense of anticipation she'd maintained despite his persistent absence. Just when she was getting used to seeing him around—just when she was looking forward to seeing him—he disappeared.

Much like her lipstick. Kassidy grimaced at the damage her teeth had done, then picked up the gold tube and smoothed on some more color. He was probably off on one of his lonely hikes. Not that it mattered one way or the other, she tried to tell herself. Matt's life was none of her business.

But she wished he'd be a little more consistent in his appearances. Not knowing when or where he'd pop up next was murder.

Kassidy heard Marla get the door. Checking the ribbon that captured her black curls and held them on top of her head, Kassidy snagged her evening bag from the table and left the bedroom

"Ready to go, gorgeous?"

"Only if I don't have to sit in Toby's car seat," she said to the man with his arm around Marla's waist. "The last time I hitched a ride with you two, I ended up with peanut butter on my tush and a sucker in my hair." Kassidy crossed the living room to give Stan a peck on the cheek, then suggested that he might want to wipe the lipstick smudge from his face, because it certainly didn't match Marla's dress. After all, he *was* Marla's date.

Following the pair out the front door, she listened to a detailed explanation of where Stan's son was spending the night. It seemed that Toby, his three-year-old son, of whom he had custody after a messy divorce, wanted to spend the night with Stan's sister, but had first insisted upon visiting his grandparents. There was also something about swinging by the mall for a quick pass through the toy store, but Kassidy couldn't swear to it.

The point of the story, it seemed, was that Toby's car seat was with Toby. Kassidy was relieved and grateful for the ride, as her date had contracted a virus, making him a no-show.

"I even cleaned the car." Stan helped Marla pile her red satin skirt into the front seat before opening the back door for Kassidy.

Kassidy stuck her head inside, scrutinizing the interior before committing herself. With a relieved sigh, she gathered her skirts around her knees and climbed in.

"You mentioned something about Matt being there tonight," Marla said. "I thought he wouldn't be caught dead at functions like this."

"People change," Kassidy returned, smiling a little as she remembered the lingerie. "I guess he decided it wouldn't kill him to show a little support. And besides, he only said he'd be here. He might have changed his mind."

"Seems like you've been seeing a lot of him lately," Marla went on, "particularly since you spent that weekend at the hotel. Anything you might have missed telling me?"

"Don't answer that, Kassidy," Stan commanded, shooting a reproving glance at Marla. "What you and Matt do is none of our business."

"We didn't *do* anything!" she fussed, finding more innuendo in Stan's observation than Marla's question. Funny how your friends thought your love life was fodder for discussion, especially when those same friends refused to do more than smile when asked similar questions.

"I didn't say you did," Marla protested innocently. "It's just that he's always hanging around you these days."

"Coincidence," Kassidy declared, wishing she hadn't told Marla anything about her bizarre week. "After all, we live in the same town and have a lot of the same friends. He's probably always been there, and I just didn't notice." She didn't mention that she hadn't seen Matt in a week. Somehow she figured that would negate her entire argument.

"Hogwash." But Stan's opinion failed to make a dent in her self-proclaimed innocence, and Kassidy determinedly ignored the laughter from the front seat.

HE WAS WAITING when they pulled up to the brilliantly lighted entrance of the hotel. Kassidy spotted him just moments before the car braked to a halt and wondered how a woman could keep such a magnificent specimen as Matt waiting.

His date must have oatmeal for brains, Kassidy deduced, because if he'd looked terrific in a tux at four, he was nothing less than sensational at thirty-three. The elegant cut of the dinner jacket did nothing to diminish his inherent ruggedness. In fact, the evening clothes did more to accent his totally masculine build than anything she'd ever seen him wear.

To be sure, Kassidy had never seen him in a suit, much less a tux, and the sight took her breath away. She had precious few seconds to get it back before he strolled over to open her door. Her attempt was only partially successful, because the closer he got, the better he looked. She watched as he pulled open the car door, felt her skin warm under his appreciative gaze. His smile was all male, his eyes raking her bare skin from shoulder to fingertip before coming to rest on the swell of her breasts above the tight bodice.

Kassidy swallowed hard, wishing the duo in the front seat would say something to break the tension. They didn't, but then, perhaps only a short second had passed, not the eons she imagined.

Matt held out his hand, waiting until she placed her own in his cool palm before speaking. "If I'd known you couldn't get a date, I would have picked you up."

Crashing back to earth to the accompaniment of uninhibited howls of laughter from the front seat, Kassidy jerked her hand free of his grasp. "Matthew Hill," she said coolly, determined not to let him get the better of her, "you have no couth."

"And your grammar is atrocious," he shot back. "Couth is an adjective—meaning sophisticated, if I'm not mistaken."

"And you're obviously very familiar with your shortcomings," she quipped to another burst of laughter from Marla and Stan. Then she and Matt shared grins of sheer pleasure as Stan rushed around to help Marla from the car.

Ignoring Matt's offer of assistance—mostly because she figured she could manage without the heat of his hand distracting her—Kassidy gathered her skirt in both hands and prepared to climb unaided from the back seat. Only it didn't go as planned, because as she pushed out one leg to step daintily onto the sidewalk, her skirt bunched even higher, revealing a long length of thigh and showing off her silk stockings and lacy garter.

At first she didn't notice. She was too busy trying to keep the heel of her other shoe from tangling in her hem to pay attention to what was already out of the car.

Matt noticed. It was all he could do not to reach out and touch, feel the proof of what his eyes couldn't believe. Kassidy was wearing sexy lingerie, and he might have gone all night without knowing.

Using his body to shield her exposure from the general public, Matt waited a long moment before she finally quit fussing with her gown and lifted her head. "This is going to make dancing with you infinitely more interesting," he said quietly, leading her gaze down to her exposed thigh.

She gasped, felt herself blush beet red and shoved the recalcitrant skirt over her knees. "Who said I'd dance with you?" she demanded, praying he wouldn't feel the tremors of excitement as he reached forward to pull her out of the car. "Your date will probably reserve that pleasure for herself."

"My date ran off with her producer last night," he muttered. "What's your excuse?"

"The plague," she breathed, suddenly aware he'd been waiting outside the hotel, just for her. That hadn't occurred to her before, even when he'd come forward to help her. She'd imagined he was waiting for his date, probably the blond Amazon. Knowing he'd been there just for her was heady stuff. Intoxicating.

"Norman's got the plague?" he asked, amused by her seeming lack of concern.

"Not Norman," she said. "Andrew. And it's probably not the plague, but it might as well be. He described the symptoms in gruesome detail when he called this afternoon. I didn't realize you were dating a starlet," she finished in the same breath.

"Not anymore." He refused to rise to the bait, satisfying himself with shooting Kassidy a look of warning before tucking her hand into the crook of his arm. They joined Stan and Marla at the door and proceeded to the ballroom entrance.

Kassidy barely managed to get in the door before she loosed the rein on her tongue. She positively *had* to know why Matt had been there to meet her, even if she hated the answer.

"How come you—?" was as far as she got, because Matt pinched her fingers, then signaled with comically raised eyebrows toward Stan and Marla.

Stan, at least, seemed to be on the ball. "Don't mind us, kids. We're going to take advantage of the bar." Marla, however, refused to budge, clearly being much more interested in the byplay between Kassidy and Matt than was politely acceptable. When Stan's attempts to divert her attention failed miserably, he shouldered the responsibility and plucked the protesting Marla from the immediate vicinity, totally oblivious of the interested bystanders, who might have challenged his right to carry his date across the ballroom.

"You were saying, honey?" Matt asked, pulling his gaze from the commotion Stan was generating. Looking into her upraised face, he wondered once again how he'd ever thought he could live without her.

She was his life. His love.

"Were you really waiting out there just for me, Matt?" she asked softly, accidentally brushing against him as they were buffeted by the incoming crowd. "Because if you were, then that was a worse idea than almost kissing me the other night."

"Why is that?" He steadied her with one hand at the small of her back and the other wrapped around the silken flesh of her arm, holding her close as they stood toe-to-toe in the ballroom's entryway. He didn't attempt to move aside, taking the excuse of the incoming crowd to hold her against him.

"Because I know the last thing you want is to have to deal with an emotional ex-wife, not to mention that it's the last thing I want to be, but I can't help it if the memories keep getting in the way of the facts." She sighed, frowning as she studied his familiar face with renewed intensity. The upheaval she'd experienced this past week was odd.

Odd, and very untimely. It was almost as though she felt the pain of their divorce now, over a year later, more than in the beginning.

Matt smiled at her gently, seeing the emotion in her eyes and finding it nearly impossible to ignore. But he had to, because that kind of emotion wouldn't solve their problems. "How was I supposed to know Warren would stand you up, honey?"

"Andrew," she corrected automatically, although why it should matter to her, she didn't know. "And he didn't stand me up. It was—"

"I know. The plague."

"So you weren't waiting for me." Strange how bereft that made her feel, Kassidy thought, wishing she could lash her foolish imagination in punishment. It suddenly became important to smile at Matt, to fool him into believing she'd only been joking. "What a pity," she said and sighed theatrically. "The salesgirl guaranteed me this dress was good for at least ten propositions tonight. If you're not going to be a notch on my belt, the least you can do is introduce me to a worthy victim."

"Don't worry about notching your belt or whatever tonight. *I'll* give you ten propositions, honey," he threatened darkly, his melodramatic visage bringing a genuine smile back to her face. "You owe me that much."

"Why?"

"Because if you'd worn silk and lace when we were married, the honeymoon might have lasted longer than six months." And then, because he couldn't afford to dwell upon that, he dropped a light kiss onto her parted lips. Withdrawing just millimeters, he reminded her, "Just me, no one else."

Kassidy pretended to think about it, but her senses were too aroused to feign indifference. "Does that mean you'll sit with me for dinner?" she asked, daring to let her palm rest on his crisp shirt. But even with the steady beat of his heart under her fingers, she wondered if this would turn out to be a fairy tale where the goblin ate the dragon. It couldn't be anything else, not in any real sense.

They were divorced.

"It means I won't let anyone else get that close," he growled, his gaze searching deep into her soul as though he could divine her thoughts . . . her true desires.

Spending the evening with her at his side wasn't what he'd planned. When his date had canceled, Matt had decided that skipping the function wouldn't accomplish anything. He wanted Kassidy to see him, to keep remembering. And even though she would be with another man, Matt had intended to remain on the periphery of her vision, intruding only once or twice for a dance or a drink.

He'd never intended to be holding her as though he couldn't let go. Hoping this one deviation wouldn't ruin his plans, Matt reminded himself that flexibility was the key to many a great strategy. Slipping his hand from her waist, he lifted her hand from his chest and placed it respectably in the crook of his elbow. And then, after reassuring himself that she wasn't about to slip away, Matt began a leisurely stroll across the room, heading in the approximate direction of one of the many bars.

"Shall we have a drink first?" he asked, lifting a couple of flutes of champagne from the bar and pressing one into Kassidy's palm.

"First?" Without stopping for the traditional toast, Kassidy poured a goodly amount of the sparkling wine down her throat. Under Matt's amused gaze, she flushed, more she supposed, from her nerves than from the alcohol.

"First," he said. "Before we dance."

"But the dancing doesn't begin until after dinner," she pointed out, gesturing to the dance floor, where groups of guests huddled together in shifting numbers.

"Don't you hear the music?"

Cocking her head to one side as though she were deaf in one ear, Kassidy concentrated. A few bars of elevator music drifted into her ears, punctuated by laughter from the fluctuating clusters of guests.

"You call *that* music?" she asked, grinning at Matt in total disbelief.

"Not music," he admitted. "More of an excuse."

"When have you ever needed an excuse?" she asked softly, relinquishing her glass to him.

"Just tonight." Slipping both glasses onto a table, he took her into his arms, and danced her onto the parquet floor.

It had been a long time since she'd danced with him, she thought. Eons had passed, it seemed, since they'd moved together to the music, their arms holding their bodies together. She loved to dance, and so did he. Alone in their house, they'd danced to music so slow they'd barely moved.

She missed it.

Dancing was something new to add to her list of regrets. Ever since they'd parted, it seemed as though the list grew, each day bringing another reminder of the things that had been good. Despite their differences, they'd still managed to share so much. Things like old movies, stale popcorn and walking in the rain. And the children, of course. Their lives had been filled with them.

She missed those things, almost as much as she missed the love they'd shared. But emotions had reigned over logic, sending them into a mad spiral that had begun with love and attraction and ended in a flaming finish of regret.

The talk about divorce had focused solely on the conflicts, downplaying the positive side—or what had been left of it by then. Divorce hadn't so much been a decision as a desperate grab for peace. They'd agreed it was best if she filed the divorce papers—she was so much better at paperwork than he. Now, from a point in time that was unaffected by the hurt, Kassidy was beginning to see that divorcing Matt was one of the stupidest decisions she'd ever made.

But it was over and done with, and dancing cheek to cheek with Matt probably wasn't in her best interests. She tried to pull herself away from the warm friction of his body, but he resisted, holding her startled gaze with his own as he waited with an impassive expression for her to object verbally.

"I don't know why you feel the need to hold me so close when the air conditioning in here seems to have gone on the fritz," she chided, pressing her palm against his chest in another attempt to put some space between them.

"Don't be silly, Kassidy," he admonished. "If we dance like you suggest, everyone here will think we're married."

"Excuse me?" Shaking her head in an attempt to restore logical thinking, she stopped dancing to stare curiously into his sherry gaze.

"I have it on good authority that married people rarely get this close, especially in public," he said with a straight face. "Dancing hip to hip, so to speak, they'll only imagine we're lovers. Surely that's better than being married?" And when she didn't respond, he prodded, "Isn't it, Kassidy? Didn't we have better luck as lovers than as husband and wife?"

Her soft gasp didn't escape him, and he absorbed it as readily as the wine. This *really* wasn't according to his plan, this dance . . . her lingerie . . .

But he didn't care. He was shooting for another chance at marriage with the woman he loved.

Tonight, in his weakness, he merely wanted her love.

4

"OUCH! Kassidy! Dammit, back off! That's my *foot* you're dancing on!" Howling his indignation, Matt hopped back and lifted his foot to check for broken toes.

Kassidy was impressed. It was testimony to his devotion to exercise and sports that Matt was able to stand one-legged in the middle of a dance floor with his injured foot cradled in his hands. But he wasn't exactly standing, she allowed. It was more of a hop, flamingo style. And he did it well.

She was also awed by his ability to ignore the snickering comments that were floating in the air around them. He wasn't even embarrassed, she noted. He was too busy checking for broken bones.

Maybe if she pushed him down onto his butt, he'd lose some more of that damned composure of his. Hopping up and down on one foot inside a crowded ballroom wasn't enough—Kassidy wanted to rattle his cage as badly as he'd rattled hers. She was angry with Matt, annoyed that he was making her remember all those things she needed so desperately to forget . . . frightened that she might not ever be able to do it.

"Damn!" he said again, a shade quieter this time.

Perhaps he was getting a bit winded from the exercise. But she knew better when she detected a steady hum of indecipherable mutterings coming from his direction. No matter. She didn't think Matt knew any words that might embarrass either of them. At least he'd never used any around her.

Kassidy noticed he was hopping in precise counterpoint to the music. He always did have an excellent sense of rhythm, she acknowledged, wishing that for once his equally remarkable sense of balance would fail him.

Seeing something other than the cheerfully friendly grin on his face told her she'd more than gotten even. The scowl he shot in her direction was stimulating, for reasons Kassidy couldn't begin to decipher.

"It'll be your fault if I miss the game tomorrow," he growled, rubbing his toes through the soft leather. "I'll be lucky if I'm not crippled."

"I'm sure you didn't hurt anything important," she said without an ounce of sympathy.

"*I* didn't hurt anything! *You're* the one who mashed her heel into my shoe!" he pointed out, cautiously lowering the bruised foot to the floor. Matt stared down at it, contemplating the gash her heel had left in the Italian leather.

"Sorry, Matt. I guess I wasn't paying attention," she said sweetly. The anger had felt good, she admitted, much better than the senseless anticipation she'd experienced all week. Anger was an emotion she could understand. She kind of hated to let it go, but it was too late. She could feel the remnants slipping away, exposing her to the less appealing emotions she'd been avoiding...confusing emotions that Matt's constant presence had produced.

"Why do I get the feeling that's a plus in my favor?" he asked, limping only slightly as he reduced the distance between them. Suspicion lighted his eyes as he narrowed his gaze upon her face. "I dread to think what might have happened if you'd had a chance to think about it."

"Perhaps if you were more careful about making such rash statements, I'd be able to concentrate on my dancing."

"I only said that we had better luck as lovers—"

"I *know* what you said, Matthew Hill!" she interrupted, outraged by his persistent reference to their past relationship. Her own equilibrium was shattering with each breath, the delicate wall she'd erected to shield her feelings from the pain of separation from Matt crumbling with little resistance.

Kassidy figured Matt knew she still loved him. She just didn't want him to think she couldn't control her love. A casual discussion of the intimacies of their marriage was definitely not constructive. She needed to forget, not remember.

"I just don't think we need to talk about things like that, Matt," she finally said, wincing at the exceedingly prissy feeling her words evoked.

"Why not?" he asked gently, smoothing his palm over the naked flesh of her arm. "I'm not suggesting anything, honey. I was just pointing out the facts. As lovers we were terrific. It was the marriage—the act of living together—that botched things up between us." His eyes narrowed again as she shivered, his fingers sensing the tiny change in her skin as she reacted to him.

"How can you say that? We were only lovers for a couple of weeks before we married," she insisted, drawn into the argument despite herself.

"We didn't stop being lovers just because we got married, Kassidy," he chided gently. "We only stopped being lovers when we divorced."

Out of the corner of one eye, Matt noticed the attention they'd drawn had been sidetracked by a commotion at the other end of the room. He took advantage of their privacy to pull her back into his arms, his breath disturbing a wisp of hair at her temple as she hesitantly leaned into him. He watched the softly curling strand settle, fascinated by the way it reflected the light from the overhead chandeliers.

"You're confusing me again, Matt," she finally said, her voice quavering over the words. "It seems like I've been confused for weeks now and I don't know why."

"That's okay, honey. I've decided tonight doesn't count, anyway."

"Excuse me?"

"I meant that since we weren't supposed to be here—together, that is—we might as well just flow with it. It really won't make any difference in the end." And it wouldn't, Matt decided. Whether they ended the evening together or not, it would have no bearing on their reconciliation—the outcome would be the same.

"And that's supposed to clarify things?"

"Not really." He sighed. "Does it matter?"

No, really it didn't. Kassidy didn't care any longer. She was too bemused by his nearness, by the way his hands warmed her through the silken fabric at the curve of her back.

But she wanted to know one thing . . . for the sake of her own sanity.

"No, Matt, it doesn't matter," she murmured. "But I need you to answer one more question. Properly, I mean."

"If you'll finish the dance with me." And he began to move slowly, not arguing when she drew back a few inches to look him in the eye. He smiled, luxuriating in the heat of her palms as they lay flat against his chest.

"We're dancing now, Matt," she prodded quietly, holding his gaze with her own. "I want my answer." Looking into those familiar eyes and seeing her own reflection gave her an odd feeling. Could he see his own as well? she wondered. Or did he see the things she was trying to hide—like the realization that her life was suddenly spiraling out of control?

"So ask your question, love," he prompted her. "And remember. You only get one. Make it count."

But his warning only made her more curious, causing her to speak before she considered her words. "Why do I get the feeling something between us is changing?"

"Because it is," Matt said gently, lifting a finger to brush aside a curl before dropping a light kiss onto her heated cheek. She was blushing. His blood pounded unevenly through his heart, making all but the simplest words impossible.

"How?" she asked, her lips hovering over the word, as though afraid to let it go.

He shook his head. "That's two questions." Then he lifted her palms from his chest to his shoulders and pulled her warmly against him. "Now we dance."

THE SPEAKER DRONED on and on and on. Kassidy was impatient, almost frantic for the dinner to be over.

When it was over, Matt had promised her another dance . . . and more. She shivered in anticipation, swallowing carefully as she tried to regain a sense of reality about what was happening to her.

But it was no use. Matt was just a few inches away, teasing her with his presence as he tempted her senses with forbidden promises. A touch here, a look there . . . he made it seem possible to hope.

Hope. She was filled with it. *Didn't we have better luck as lovers than as husband and wife?* Had he really said it . . . and what was he trying to tell her? Kassidy shivered again, wishing she could just turn and ask him flat out if he thought they should become lovers.

But she couldn't, because she was afraid he'd say no, afraid it was all a figment of her imagination, a fantasy she'd created to satisfy her own longings.

Would being Matt's lover satisfy the emptiness inside?
She puzzled over that, wondering when she'd become aware
that something was missing from her very full life. But she
couldn't place the onset of the strangely forlorn sensation
and tried to put it aside. Casting a sideways glance at Matt,
Kassidy tried to imagine what he was really thinking. He
looked so cool, so controlled.

Perhaps all he really wanted was another dance. She
sighed, acutely aware of the sensual rub of the nylon stockings as she uncrossed her legs under the table. The sensation was delicious, and it was all she could do to keep a
straight face.

The lingerie had been an impulse, and Kassidy was mature enough to admit that she hadn't bought it solely for her
own pleasure. Somewhere deep inside, she'd known Matt
would approve. And somehow Matt's approval had become important to her. Not that she'd ever admit it to him.

Now Kassidy had the bonus of knowing Matt did approve. The hot look in his eyes as he'd stared at the garters
had reminded her of the Matt she used to know.

Yes, Matt had been right about the lingerie.

Matt had been right about other things, as well—her car,
for instance. The maintenance bills were soaring, and it was
in such disreputable shape that her boss had threatened to
have it towed from the lot at work while she wasn't looking. She hadn't impressed him much with her protest that
it could drive to the junkyard under its own steam. Matt had
been right about the advantages of driving a relatively new
car, she conceded, even if he was more concerned with aes-
thetics than function.

Maybe next month, she mused. She'd squeeze out a few
extra dollars from the new promotion and elevate her standards in transportation. But in the meantime she'd splurged

on lingerie. Her thoughts drifted back to his startling statement about their success as lovers.

Lovers. It had never occurred to her they could recapture the one thing that hadn't provided fuel for their arguments. And if that was a fantasy, then Matt made her want to believe in it.

She must be out of her mind! Kassidy shook her head in an attempt to discipline her errant thoughts, disturbing the soft curls at her forehead. It must be the moon, she decided, lifting her fingers to pat the curls back into place. Her imagination was running wild. Tomorrow she'd be back to normal, she promised herself . . . and wondered why that prospect seemed so dismal.

"I knew there was a reason I hated these things," Matt murmured, catching her off guard as he leaned close. "This guy is *never* going to quit!"

Matt's whisper nearly provoked a giggle, but Kassidy hastily smothered it with the linen napkin from her lap. The napkin was a good strategy, because it also muffled the gasp of pleasure that escaped when he nibbled lightly at her ear before settling back into his own chair.

Matt heard the shallow breathing she couldn't control because he was listening for it. Her ears had always been particularly sensitive, he remembered, and he supposed he shouldn't have given in to his impulse for a quick tease.

But fair play wasn't on his mind tonight. Kassidy was beside him, aware of him as she hadn't been since they'd parted a year ago, and Matt didn't intend to surrender the advantage.

He wanted her, and he needed her to want him. And if he could have what he wanted tonight, perhaps the rest would come more easily.

But no, he knew better than that. Had it been easy, they would have succeeded the first time. Matt cleared his throat, letting his gaze rest blankly on the man at the podium as he considered the night ahead.

"I know you aren't up to speed on protocol, but this is the part where you're supposed to put your hands together and make loud, clapping noises. It's called applause."

Matt's head whipped sideways as Kassidy spoke, then back to the podium where the speaker was accepting the surprisingly enthusiastic accolade of the audience. Too deeply entrenched in his own thoughts, Matt had obviously missed what must have been a stirring conclusion.

He really didn't mind. Grinning as he raised his hands to applaud the end if not the content of the speech, Matt added his praise to the rest. Kassidy was laughing at him, of course, her eyes aglow with mirth as she chuckled beneath the applause. It was too much to expect that she'd overlook his lapse of attention—not when he'd already done his best to divert hers.

"What about that dance you promised me?"

Flashing an intoxicating smile in his direction, Kassidy rose from her chair and held out her hand, palm open. Matt stared at her palm, carefully shielding what he knew was a white-hot flash of desire behind shuttered eyes. It was all he could do not to press his lips to that sensitive place just below her thumb . . . to show her how her laughing initiative affected him.

Instead, Matt curled his fingers around hers and allowed Kassidy to pull him to his feet. They were in the process of excusing themselves from their dinner companions when Marla and Stan wandered over from their own table.

"Are you guys going to mingle a little tonight or what?" Marla asked, smirking as she subjected the couple to an amused examination.

Not knowing why she should feel guilty, Kassidy watched Marla's eyes pause on the hand she still linked with Matt's.

Her fingers wriggled as she halfheartedly attempted to break the contact, but Matt wasn't cooperating. The swift glance she stole at his clear, unspeaking gaze was explicit. He didn't want to let go.

She abandoned her meager attempts to escape his touch and was rewarded by a quick squeeze of his fingers. Kassidy sighed, returning Marla's quizzical look with an innocent shrug, trying to get used to the feel of Matt's fingers around hers.

"We were headed for the dance floor," Matt said with an easy smile, ignoring Marla's opening gambit. "But I could easily be persuaded to change partners for a few moments, if Stan wouldn't mind." Stan cheerfully agreed to switch and Matt was suddenly handing Kassidy to Stan as he reached for Marla.

A bit dazed by the speed of the change, Kassidy watched as Matt and Marla threaded their way through the tables toward the dance floor where the band was segueing into a jazzy version of a popular song. They were laughing hysterically, obviously sharing a joke as Matt swung Marla into the crowd.

She hadn't been ready to let go, not yet.

"You're not supposed to look at your ex-husband like that," Stan pointed out. "Everyone will think you still care."

"Of course I care," she murmured, her attention focused on the dance floor. "We got divorced because we couldn't live together, not because we didn't care."

When Stan didn't have anything to say to that, Kassidy quit trying to follow the occasional flash of Matt's blond hair amid the dancers and looked up at her partner. "Does that surprise you?"

"A little," he admitted, taking her elbow then to guide her to the back of the room and into the foyer. It was quieter there, and they began walking slowly toward the far end.

Stan waited until they were more or less alone before he continued. "I guess I always believed love could make anything possible."

"Sorry to disappoint you," she said flatly, "but it doesn't work that way."

"Not for you, at least."

That grated a little, but she tried not to let it show. "We weren't a good match," she said, trying to explain what she'd never really understood herself. "There's too much different about us, too much we don't like about each other."

"Which explains why you're still mooning after him," Stan offered, ducking the blow Kassidy aimed at his shoulder.

"I am not *mooning* over him," she denied vehemently, stomping a few feet ahead before turning back to face Stan. "I may love him, but I'd never moon over him!"

Stan just stood there grinning at her, then changed the subject to stories about his son, which delighted Kassidy. Listening to tales of Toby's escapades never failed to amuse her, and right now she wasn't in the mood to defend what she did or did not feel for Matt. The stories had reached the outrageous stage, where Kassidy knew Stan was relying more on imagination than fact, when he looked past her shoulder and raised his hand to wave.

"You'd better practice your not mooning expression, Kassidy," he told her. And he pointed across the foyer to the couple stepping off the escalator.

"I thought they were dancing," Kassidy said slowly, conscious of a vague flicker of jealousy as she watched Matt and Marla cross the expanse of red carpet.

"We were dancing," Matt said easily, having overheard Kassidy's remark. "But Marla needed to find the, er—"

"The bathroom," Marla supplied, leaving Matt's side to ease into Stan's embrace.

Kassidy looked pointedly at the rest room conveniently located across the foyer, lifting her brows in silent query as she confronted Matt's innocent gaze.

"The line was a mile long at that one," Marla added innocently. "Matt took me downstairs. I'm surprised we didn't see you when we left the ballroom."

"I guess Stan and I were too busy talking," Kassidy murmured, narrowing her eyes on Matt's suspiciously amused expression. Why did she get the feeling she was missing something here?

"And what were you and Stan discussing that was so fascinating?" Matt still held himself apart from the trio, pleasuring himself with the picture Kassidy made in her ball gown, her bare shoulders a sweet invitation for his touch. Soon, he promised himself.

"The moon," Stan responded easily as Kassidy's face suffused with color.

"I'll show you the moon, lover," Marla promised Stan as she tried to lead him back to the ballroom. "Think you two can get along without us?" she asked over her shoulder.

"We'll manage," Matt said dryly, then added, "in case we don't run into you later, I'll see Kassidy home tonight."

Stan acknowledged Matt's statement with a wave of his hand and they were gone.

Turning his gaze back to Kassidy, he said politely, "Is that all right?"

"I suppose it'll have to do," she said, gulping at the unmasked look of desire in his eyes. It seared her, made her burn with a kind of wanting she hadn't known in a year.

It gave her the courage to forget about tomorrow.

Taking a final deep breath, Kassidy drifted on legs that trembled to where Matt stood waiting. "May I have the pleasure of this dance?" she asked softly, offering her hand to him as she had once before. She waited, breathless now, as his eyes focused on her mouth. Her lips throbbed, then parted under his steady gaze.

He didn't say anything, but wrapped his fingers around hers and pulled her steadily closer, his mouth descending to within millimeters of hers before he stopped. Kassidy felt the silky caress of his breath just moments before his lips settled upon hers. A cry of joy escaped her only to be muffled within the moist cavern of his mouth, and she strained to deepen the contact.

Matt made it easy for her, dipping his head to meet the urgent need they shared, giving her his mouth without holding back. Her tongue quickly crossed the ivory ridge of his teeth, flicking across his tongue in an invitation to follow. It did, thrusting into her mouth without holding back, his hands closing on her arms to hold her still under his hungry assault.

And then, suddenly, as though startled at what he'd done, he lifted his head. Kassidy watched as he took several deep breaths, knowing that was how her own lungs were responding to the dearth of air. When he finally brought his gaze back to her face, she was smiling.

"You look like the cat that ate the canary," he murmured, releasing his grip on her forearms and massaging the reddening skin with his palms.

"I can't help it," she said, wishing for privacy to continue what the kiss had begun. "Kissing you always did put me in good humor."

"As long as you don't laugh when I start making love to you, I guess that's okay," he commented, his eyes watching hers for any sign of doubt.

Kassidy swallowed nervously, aware she'd just passed an imaginary line, knowing there could be no going back. "I won't laugh," she whispered, feeling her heart thump erratically as she returned his stare.

He nodded, then let out the breath he'd been holding. Slipping his arm around her waist, he steered her slowly toward the music. "We still haven't had our dance."

I'd rather spend the time kissing you, she thought to herself. But there was nothing for it but to allow herself to be dragged onto the dance floor, so Kassidy pretended it was a fine idea.

The music was fast, pulsing energy into the crowd that moved rhythmically to its beat. It wasn't what she would have chosen, but Kassidy didn't let that stop her from joining in, moving in counterpoint to Matt as they danced under the muted lights. The rhythm changed a little with the next song, and she laughed as Matt whooped his recognition of a sixties favorite. The crowd was in tune with the band, following the pace set by the drums, going a little wild when the sax player took center stage.

And when he'd finished, the band retreated from the frenzied pace with a slow, sensual love song that made Kassidy's heart beat even faster. She went into Matt's arms without a second thought, forgetting all her defenses, blocking out any thought of the pain tomorrow would surely bring.

They couldn't live together, she'd told Stan. It was a truth she'd learned to live with, and there was nothing to be done about it. Just as there was nothing that could keep her from wanting Matt tonight.

Matt held her carefully, guiding her through the swaying crowd as the song played itself out, not letting go when it was over because he couldn't . . . wouldn't. He was lucky, though. Another melody, as sweet as the first, poured out over the receptive crowd, and he pulled her a little closer, until her cheek was resting on his chest, his face buried in her hair.

"I've missed dancing with you," she said, her breath warming him through his linen shirt.

"You won't change your mind?" he asked, lifting her chin so he could look into her eyes as she found her answer.

He wasn't talking about dancing, and she knew it. But she couldn't resist the urge to tease him, just a little. "Why should I change my mind?" she asked, mischief clear in her expression as she deliberately misinterpreted his question. "I love dancing with you."

"I'm not talking about dancing, honey," he growled. "There's lots more at stake here than a few spins around the dance floor."

"Are you trying to talk me out of it?" she whispered.

"I just need to make sure you know."

"I know."

"It won't change anything," he said, because she had to know that making love wasn't the answer to their problems.

"I know," she said again, knowing it was a lie, but without knowing why.

5

KASSIDY STARED into the night through the enormous pane of glass that took up an entire wall of the hotel room. The view of Seattle was spectacular, almost magical, with thousands of lights fairly shimmering in the crystal-clear air of the city. Muted traffic noises drifted up from the street far below, the late-night tempo a fitting accompaniment to the vibrant city.

Refocusing, she studied the reflection of the man behind her. He moved slowly, shucking his dinner jacket to lay it across the back of a chair, before bending to flick on a small lamp. She stared at the long fingers that pulled at the bow of his tie, fascinated to discover he hadn't made do with a clip-on, wondering how long it had taken him to learn to tie it. He moved to stand within a few feet of her, close enough for her to hear his harsh breathing, the rustle of his shirt as he worked to loosen the top button. The studs came next, his fingers maintaining an unhurried rhythm that was tantalizingly provocative.

The sizzling heat of his desire was a raw force, undiminished by the fact she was watching a reflection. Kassidy gasped at the sensual tightening between her shoulder blades and found herself dipping her head forward in response to the traveling tension that started at the base of her spine and ended at the nape of her neck. The tremors that shook her were potent, even more so as she lifted her head to see Matt hadn't missed a thing.

His slow smile was a delicious acknowledgment of his recognition of what she was feeling. He paused for a moment, his fingers curling around the edges of his shirt as he let his gaze stroke the exposed skin on her back.

"I used to lie awake at night, remembering how sensitive you were there . . . on your back. It made me crazy, thinking about how excited you would become when I touched you there." He laughed then, as though discovering a new pleasure. "But I haven't touched you yet, Kassidy," he murmured, "have I?"

She didn't answer. Her throat was too dry, her lips paralyzed in the anticipation of his kiss. She hadn't spoken when they'd left the party. Not even when he produced the key to this room had she done much more than sigh in relief that the long drive home had been omitted. And now, as she waited for Matt to come to her, she could do no more than pray he'd touch her soon—before she came apart at the seams.

His eyes flared with the knowledge of her arousal, but he maintained the small distance between them. Kassidy found herself held immobile by the compelling promise of his gaze, a trembling statue that needed only his touch to come alive.

She watched his eyes as they traced the tremors between her shoulder blades, willed him to touch her there. The frustration when he didn't was as exciting as the anticipation of knowing he would . . . eventually . . . when he was ready. It wouldn't be right for her to go to him; that wasn't what he wanted. Kassidy was amazed how easily she could read his desires—the unspoken communication between lovers that set the ground rules. And, for the moment, she understood his need to be in charge.

The last stud was finally pocketed, and he pulled the shirttail from his trousers, providing her with a shadowed view of his chest. Her breathing became harsh and fast as she remembered in minute detail how it felt to brush the tips of her breasts across the softly curling hair of his chest.

But she couldn't touch, not until he was ready. Kassidy bit her bottom lip, hard, hoping the small discipline would prevent any impetuous moves on her part. Holding her gaze on the slow movements of his hands, she planned her revenge for this interminable wait.

The idea came in the form of a simple gesture. Lifting a shaky hand from her side, Kassidy pressed her fingers to the reflection of his open shirt. She heard the rapid intake of breath from behind as her palm lingered against the cool glass of the window, and knew without a doubt that she had provoked him into doing what she wanted most.

What came next was so dramatically intoxicating that she would have fallen had it not been for the arm that slipped around her waist. Kassidy shuddered as hot, wet lips slid across her shoulder to nuzzle the fine hairs at her nape. Her hand fell from the window, pausing in midair as his lips parted to allow sharp teeth a chance to nibble. Her cries were an instinctive response, the uttering of his name an involuntary plea as her fingers reached back to tangle in his hair.

He ignored her appeal even as he fulfilled her needs. The arm around her waist tightened, pulled her closer into the heat of his body as his free hand glided across her breasts, his fingers grazing the tops of those creamy mounds left exposed by her gown. Kassidy drifted on a cloud of pure pleasure, her own free hand seeking a hold on the arm at her waist, the other guiding his head as his mouth roamed her neck and shoulder. She stretched and arched, offering everything she had in exchange for the miracle of his touch, the exquisite sensation of his lips on her body.

When his fingers dipped below the fabric of her gown to torment the burgeoning nipples beneath, she cried out in relief. The stays in her gown were no defense against his determination as he pulled the silk to a point just below the rosy tips. His fingers flicked and caressed, pinched and soothed. Kassidy opened her eyes to their reflections, gasping her pleasure even as she worried about the propriety of it all.

"Are you sure we should be doing this?"

Matt pulled her tight against his hard arousal, showing her his assurance without words. "Does this feel like I have any doubts?" he asked, his breath a smooth whisper against her skin. His fingers tangled in her hair and pulled at the ribbon until it loosened and her curls fell around his hand.

Kassidy shivered, tantalized by the wet warmth of his mouth as it skated down the curve of her neck. "I mean the window," she insisted, fighting to maintain a level of reason. "If we can see out—"

"There's nobody near enough to see in," he murmured into her ear, pointing out that the nearest high rise was blocks away. "I specifically asked for this side of the building."

"And I thought this was all my idea," she teased, catching her breath as his fingers found the zipper of her gown. The pressure of the bodice beneath her nipples was relieved, freeing her breasts to fall into Matt's hands.

"It was your idea," he retorted, moving back a fraction to allow her gown to fall to the floor. "I only provided a convenient location."

"So this is what you and Marla were doing downstairs," she said, thrilled to realize he'd wanted this night as much as she. "I'd hate to think I forced you into anything," she breathed, shutting her eyes to the unbearably erotic picture of Matt's hands roaming across her belly and down to where his fingers tangled in the lacy garters. The crisp fabric of his shirt tantalizingly chafed the bare skin of her back, and Kassidy shimmied against him in voluptuous enjoyment.

Matt held his breath as she moved, squeezing his eyes closed momentarily to shut out the reflection of his hands exploring the bits of lingerie that adorned the body of the woman he loved. Making love with Kassidy was always like this—hot to the point of explosion. She responded to him with a wanton abandon that never failed to ignite his own response, drove him to the very end of his control . . . and then beyond.

Expelling a harsh breath, Matt smoothed trembling fingers over the lace at her thighs, glancing at the window to watch her face as he traced the satiny flesh left bare above the stockings. This was what had really decided him. He would have never taken the chance of making love to Kassidy, if he hadn't been convinced it was what she wanted . . . and if he hadn't believed she wanted more than this. The brief glimpse he'd had earlier, the flash of thigh as she left the car . . . that had been the first real sign of a willingness to change.

His blood boiled when he considered she'd chosen something so provocative to demonstrate this new attitude. Silk and lace against the satin of her skin.

Bracing himself to absorb the full weight of her body as she leaned into him, Matt lifted his hands to her breasts, teasing the swollen mounds for long moments before sliding down to savor the contrasting textures below. Moving in unison, his palms swept down to the silk of her stockings, feathering lightly over the delicate garters, the narrow panties cut high on her hips. Hot, determined fingers traced the line between her thighs, up and down, exerting a small, persistent pressure until she gave in to his silent demand and parted them.

He rewarded her with a gentle caress, a light stroking that might not have happened at all ... a touch that stole her breath and sent her reeling.

And when she could breathe again, it was to look up from cool, crisp sheets as Matt dealt with the remainder of his own clothes. She wasn't surprised to find herself in bed ... just grateful. Matt's sensual assault had left her weak, and watching him strip away the last of his clothes was even more stimulating. He hadn't changed, she realized. He was still the most beautiful man she'd ever seen. Firm and hard and, surprisingly, already glistening with a thin film of moisture as though he'd been working out.

"You're sweating," she murmured, gasping as he leaned over to lay his hot palm against her belly. His heat seared her, aroused her ... flung her back to the fever pitch of moments before.

"It's called control," he said, increasing the pressure of his palm without moving it. "And it'll probably get worse before it gets better."

"No reason for that!" she gasped, reaching up to trail a fingertip across his chest. "I'm not even sure I like the sound of that. Control isn't something I'm looking for tonight."

"You mean you want me inside you right now?" he whispered, fingering the hem of her panties. "No preliminaries ... no games?"

"What do you call that scene at the window?" she breathed, not quite catching her breath as his mouth descended to close over her belly button. His tongue dived hard into the small depression, his breath heated ... then cooled before he lifted his head.

"I call that an appetizer," he said, holding her eyes as his fingers plucked at the flimsy strip that banded her hips. "I haven't had you naked in a year. I intend to ... prolong the experience," he murmured, leaving the panties in place as he fingered the garters.

"I'm not exactly naked," she protested, enjoying the flare of his eyes as her fingertip traced a downward path.

"You will be." The warmth of his fingers teased the sensitive flesh at her thighs. "Eventually. But I think we'll enjoy your purchases for a bit longer."

Kassidy gasped at the erotic promise, had almost caught her breath when he wrested her finger from its teasing path down his chest and captured her hands, pressing them against the pillow beneath her head. The excitement built as she considered her options, wondering if he'd respond wildly to a carefully placed nip on his shoulder . . . or if the hollow behind his ear was still as vulnerable to a wet tongue.

But he was ahead of her, leaning forward to plunge his tongue into her mouth, again and again, until she was too weak to protest, too excited to try. And when his mouth closed over an aching nipple, she arched off the bed, falling back as Matt toyed with the lingerie at her hips, fondling and stroking as his mouth gently sucked at her breast. Kassidy gave herself up to the exquisite feeling, only half aware that her hands were free again . . . and hanging on to his shoulders as though they would never let go.

He stroked and caressed and gentled, never lessening the rhythm, always sending her higher than before. He swallowed her cries when the pleasure was too intense, then held her as she descended from the heights. He rediscovered the old Kassidy . . . and stumbled upon parts of her new self in the process. Her back was as excitingly responsive as ever, but it was the intriguing sensitivity at the inside of her elbow that drove her to new peaks of excitement.

She never knew when the rest of her clothing was removed—only that there were no longer any barriers between them. She soared when he entered into the final intimacy, screaming her joy into the welcoming cavern of his mouth as they shared the finest moments of their lives.

Loving Matt had never been quite so hot, quite so exciting.

Loving Matt had never been quite so right.

WHEN KASSIDY WOKE, she was alone.

She knew it instinctively. Matt was gone, and not just from the bed. He wasn't in the room. And he wasn't in the adjoining living room or bathroom.

Kassidy knew what it felt like to be alone, without Matt. She'd had a lot of practice during the last year.

So why did it feel so much worse now?

Impatient with the emotional reaction to what was a perfectly normal event, she rolled off the bed, ignoring her weak knees as she grabbed the hotel-provided robe and pulled it on. She was still tying the belt when she opened the door to the living room, her eyes scanning the horizontal surfaces as she looked for the note she was sure he had left.

The knock at the door interrupted her search. Grinning at the thought of finding Matt behind that door, she threw it open. A scowl overtook her expression when it wasn't Matt. The woman in the maid's uniform smiled tentatively as she handed the package she was carrying to Kassidy.

"What's this?" she asked suspiciously, leaning out the door to peek down the hallway. No Matt, she discovered. So where the hell was he?

"I'm not sure," the maid returned, backing away from the door. "The gentleman in the lobby just asked me to bring it to you."

"Just now?"

"Oh, no, ma'am," the young girl responded. "Earlier, about three hours ago, when I first came on shift. But he told me to wait until now, because you were sleeping."

Kassidy pretended to ignore the badly concealed smirk on the maid's face, choosing instead to smile her thanks and shut the door. Turning the key in the lock, she tore into the package.

It was a sweater and slacks, probably from the boutique downstairs. Flinging the garments onto a nearby chair, Kassidy paced the floor in front of the window, trying to decide if she was pleased or angry that Matt had gone to the trouble of ensuring she could walk out of the hotel in daylight without looking like a remnant of last night's party. At the very least, she had to admire his initiative. Considering he'd left at the crack of dawn, he'd probably had to bribe someone to open the shop.

She would have been happier if he'd stayed around long enough to be thanked, she finally decided. And she would have been a lot happier if he'd stayed around long enough to say good-morning, but pushed any grouchy thoughts out of her head. The last thing she wanted to feel this morning was grouchy.

Determined to avoid analyzing her feelings about waking up alone in the same bed she'd so recently shared with her ex-husband, Kassidy snagged the clothes from the chair and hauled her sore body into the shower.

All the same, not analyzing her own feelings didn't stop her from trying to figure out where he'd disappeared to. Turning on the shower, Kassidy waited a moment for the water to warm before enveloping herself in the stimulating spray. He had probably left for something like an early game, she mused as she washed her hair, remembering countless weekend mornings when Matt had been up and gone before she'd opened her eyes. Football, baseball, tennis and volleyball were only a few of the sporting activities that Matt enjoyed, and they all required some traveling if you wanted to participate in competitions. But he'd have to come back sometime.

And she'd be waiting for him.

So Kassidy focused on the practical things as she stepped out of the shower, wet and dripping onto the cool floor— things like how she was going to get from the hotel to her house. A taxi, she decided, unwilling to face the inquisition to which she knew Marla would subject her if she dared call. If she was lucky, she might be able to sneak in before Marla was up and about. Drying herself briskly on an enormous towel that was warm from the rack, she purposely cleared her mind of any thoughts about the last twelve hours— hours that had changed her life forever.

Major decisions like those that were imminent couldn't be made alone. She'd wait until later, she decided, when she could sit down with Matt and talk things through. Kassidy rummaged in her evening bag for a comb, then went to work on her freshly washed hair with the blow dryer thought- fully provided by the hotel. She hummed as she worked, fluffing the curls into a semblance of order before she quit. Satisfied with her appearance, she left the bathroom and sifted through the sheets and blankets until every scrap of lingerie was accounted for.

It only took a few moments to dress, although Kassidy felt a bit self-conscious about the glittering heels that peeked out from under the hem of her wool slacks. At least what she was wearing beneath the practical clothes didn't show, she consoled herself, even more aware of the unseen lin- gerie than the shoes. Stuffing her gown into the bag that had held the clothes she was now wearing, she stopped to check the room for anything she might have forgotten.

One glance at the thoroughly rumpled bed was enough to send her speeding through the door. Later, she promised herself as she hurried down the quiet hallway toward the elevator banks. Later she could wallow in the exciting memories of her night with Matt. Later, when his arms were around her again, lending credibility to the astonishing fantasy.

For now she concentrated on maintaining a feeling of cautious well-being. Things were changing, she told herself. Things were finally changing . . . and in a direction so unexpected that she could hardly believe her luck.

Waltzing through the lobby door and into the brilliant sunshine of a wonderfully quiet Sunday morning, Kassidy grinned at the doorman and slid into a waiting taxi.

Everything, it seemed, was going her way.

"WHAT DO YOU MEAN, he's gone?" Kassidy's fingers tightened around the phone; things weren't going as expected. But her growing anger was clearly lost on the person at the other end of the line.

"He stopped by here on his way out," the clerk at Matt's store replied. "He picked up that new portable stove and said he'd be back in a week."

"He went hiking?" She couldn't believe it, didn't want to believe it.

"Yes, Ms Canyon. I think he said he was headed to Mt. Baker National Forest, somewhere around Whitechuck Mountain. Do you want me to check that for you? I imagine he left the details with Roger."

As if there were anything she could do about it, Kassidy fumed. What did he expect, that she would go into the wilderness and look for him? Reminding herself that killing the bearer of bad news was not a socially accepted practice, she kept a tight rein on her temper and managed to hang up without making a huge fool of herself.

Making a *small* fool out of herself had been unavoidable. After all, it probably wasn't every day that the boss's ex-wife called, demanding to know where her former husband was hiding. But after spending an entire day waiting for him to call, long, fruitless hours at her office, where she'd attempted to get a head start on Monday's barrage, Kassidy had given in to the need to know.

At least she'd not succumbed to the temptation to wait for him at his house.

A week. Plunking down her forehead onto arms that were crossed atop the pile of papers she'd been studying, Kassidy took several deep breaths. When the fury didn't subside, she moved her arms and banged her head repeatedly on the poorly cushioned desk. The solid thud wasn't so much painful as startlingly loud in the deserted office, and the empty sound of the echoes reverberated in the stillness surrounding her.

A final thud produced the most meaningful result, and Kassidy lifted her head to gingerly rub the tender spot just above her left eye. "Damn that impossible man!" she raged, adding a few unrepeatable adjectives for good measure. If he thought he could seduce her and then just walk out, he had another think coming!

Although Kassidy knew that she'd technically had as much to do with the seduction as Matt, it didn't change anything. She'd woken that morning, tingling with excitement, euphoric about their future . . . never for a moment dreaming that Matt wouldn't share her optimism.

"*It won't change anything,*" he'd said last night. And she'd agreed.

"So I changed my mind," Kassidy said aloud, ignoring the tinge of guilt that implied she wasn't being strictly honest with herself. If she was being honest, it was more a case of having told the fib last night rather than today. She'd known that making love with her ex-husband would change everything.

The anger faded, and the emotion it had masked was suddenly overwhelming in its force. *She loved him.* She'd always known that, but now it was different. Now, a year after their divorce, she was beginning to realize that she would never let go of that love. The only thing that living without him had accomplished was to make her thoroughly miserable.

She loved him, and she wanted him back. Leaning against the padded vinyl back of her chair, Kassidy threw her feet up and onto the desk and scowled at the charcoal drawing in the pewter frame next to the telephone. The drawing was at once simple and stunningly arresting. A single deer grazed in a meadow deep with summer's grass, a breeze caressed the leaves of nearby aspen, the sun kissed the late-blooming wildflowers. You could see it all, imagine the colors . . . feel the breeze.

Kassidy felt her loneliness abate as she remembered the day Matt had sketched the scene, could almost feel his pleasure when she'd dragged him all over town, looking for just the right frame. It was a masterpiece, she'd said, the best he'd ever done. And Matt had laughed it off, saying his sketches and drawings weren't meant to be great, that he enjoyed doing them, reliving with his pencil the enchantment he found in the out-of-doors.

Kassidy didn't want that tiny drawing to be the only thing she had of Matt. She wanted him, the man, her love.

But what about the arguments? a tiny voice inside her asked. *The fights, the battles?* What had happened between them that would make things better . . . would make their marriage work this time? Why did she think they had a chance, now, a year after their divorce, when essentially nothing had changed?

It really didn't matter, she decided, firmly ignoring the questions so that she wouldn't have to deal with their answers. What was important now was that she loved him, needed him. Busy though she kept herself, life without Matt had been horribly empty, and she couldn't see the sense in continuing the status quo.

It would work because they wanted it to.

All she had to do now was convince Matt. *"It won't change anything,"* he'd insisted. But did he really believe that? Perhaps that was why he'd felt the need to put an entire wilderness between them—he was taking a time-out to rethink his position. Kassidy pondered that idea, becoming more convinced by the second that he'd only retreated, and that he'd return. Her best-case scenario had him coming back, wanting to resume their marriage and live happily ever after. At the worst, he might try to convince himself that nothing had happened at all.

More likely, though, Matt would be unsure what he wanted to do about Kassidy, about them. But that was all right with her.

Kassidy was sure.

Staring somewhat cross-eyed at the old-fashioned bank of clocks at the end of the room over the ticker board, Kassidy noticed it was almost time for breakfast in Hong Kong. Her stomach rumbled in response to the thought of eggs and bacon as she sifted through various plans. He'd have to know she was serious about this, she decided. That would take some pretty overt moves on her part. Mooning after him would get her nowhere, although Stan and everyone else would have a pretty good idea what was going through her head.

Letting him know her intentions was going to be easy, albeit a tad underhanded. She smiled as she thought how Matt might react. But what happened next stumped her, and Kassidy invented and rejected several alternatives before

deciding *not* to decide. Best to concentrate on step one and
let the rest follow naturally, she resolved.

And, she determined, overt action was best accomplished on a full stomach. Reaching into her open purse,
Kassidy pulled out a package of Twinkies and the bologna
sandwich she'd made that morning. Stuffing half the Twin-
kie into her mouth, she leaned back in her chair, opened the
center drawer of her desk and slid the papers she'd been
studying into the void. And then, as nervous excitement
roiled her stomach, she picked up the phone and dialed her
mother's number.

On the off chance that Matt was able to convince himself
their night together had changed nothing, Kassidy was determined to prove him wrong. This was going to be especially effective if everyone else knew the exact opposite.
Laughing aloud with almost wicked delight, she prepared
a mental list of calls she intended to make. As the ring of a
distant telephone sounded in her ear, Kassidy rehearsed the
words she'd use to inform friends and family of the new—
renewed—intimacy between Matt and herself.

She knew how she was going to get him back. Unfortunately, she still didn't know how she was going to keep him.
Kassidy focused solely on the silver lining, refusing to ac-
knowledge the black cloud beneath it.

"IF YOU WERE PREGNANT, I could understand your attitude," Amanda Canyon protested as she poured herself another cup of coffee. "But you've only slept with the man
once in the last year—"

"Doesn't talking about my sex life embarrass you at all?"
Kassidy interrupted, reaching across the kitchen table to
pull another doughnut out of the box.

"You brought up the subject," her mother said saucily,
shuddering delicately as Kassidy closed her mouth over her

third jelly-filled doughnut. A shorter and somewhat plumper version of her daughter, Amanda Canyon could never comprehend how Kassidy kept her weight under control so easily. The food that went into her mouth rarely had more than a passing acquaintance with nutrition, and regular eating habits were an unknown quality. But long ago she'd decided it was something to do with her daughter's metabolism and the breakneck pace Kassidy had always maintained. "Besides, I'd rather talk about your sex life than a lot of other things."

"What other things?" Kassidy asked, her words somewhat garbled.

"Like why it's been three months since you've come to visit your mother, for a start," Amanda Canyon said. "And if you tell me it's because you've been working—"

"But I have!"

"And you can't take one weekend off to drive thirty miles?" Shaking her head disparagingly, she continued. "No wonder your marriage didn't last. You probably spent more time commuting to work than you did in bed."

"So we're back to bed, are we?" Kassidy grinned as she licked away the sugar that stuck to her lips.

"Looks like it," her mother agreed. "Back to my question. What makes you think you can use one night's folly to force Matt to marry you?"

"In the first place, I'm not in the least sure I'm *not* pregnant," Kassidy said, laughing out loud at her mother's unashamedly hopeful expression. Amanda Canyon rarely exhibited a traditional streak, but it appeared she found the notion of another grandchild rather appealing. Kassidy didn't pursue that topic, mostly because she had other priorities. "And in the second place, I wouldn't dream of using that kind of bribery."

"So why have you been broadcasting your indiscretion all over Puget Sound if you don't want to force him into marrying you?"

"Marrying me *again*," Kassidy corrected her. "That's important to remember. It's not like I'm trying to trap a man who's never shown an interest in living with me. I won't demand marriage if I'm pregnant, but I'll use everything I know to make him realize we belong together."

"I still don't understand," her mother said with a sigh. "What on earth are you accomplishing by letting everyone know you're still attracted to your ex-husband? Don't you think it's a little tacky?"

"As far as the rest of the world is concerned, nothing," she admitted, sipping her hot chocolate. "But with everyone watching, Matt won't be able to turn his back on the situation. He'll have to deal with it . . . with me."

"And what if you're wrong?" Amanda Canyon proposed. "What if he comes back from that camping trip, intending to give your marriage another chance, and finds all your friends gossiping about how you spent the night together? Don't you think he'll be the least bit miffed by having his private life broadcast all over the Northwest?"

"Then that'll teach him not to kiss and run," Kassidy returned bravely. More bravely than she felt. Five days into her campaign to advertise her renewed relationship with Matt, she was increasingly nervous about his reaction. And he was due back tomorrow, she knew, in time for the Saturday Little League game.

Amanda Canyon just snorted her disbelief and opened the oven to poke a fork into the roast that was sizzling inside. Returning to her chair at the oilcloth-covered table, she faced her daughter. "Are you sure you're doing the right thing, Kassidy?"

"Calling all our friends?" she asked, thinking they'd already exhausted the subject.

"I meant you and Matt," Amanda said, her concern obvious by the expression on her face. "Tactics aside, I wonder if you've thought out the difficulties of what you're trying to accomplish. Just because you want your marriage to work doesn't mean it will."

"Of course I've thought it out," Kassidy retorted, carefully ignoring the sudden tightening of sensitive nerves. "We'll both have to try harder not to fight this time. That's where we blew it last time, the fighting."

"And just how do you propose to get rid of the arguments?" Amanda asked softly.

"We can do anything we set our minds to," Kassidy said, not daring to look into Amanda's eyes, because she didn't want to see the skepticism she knew she'd find. "If we decide not to fight, we won't." She felt a niggling sense of disquiet, but stubbornly refused to give in to it, holding her ground because she so much wanted to believe she had the answers.

"I guess we'll see then," Amanda replied, her disappointment plain as she pushed herself up from the table to check her dinner.

"Mom, I really do love him," Kassidy said to her mother's back, aware that her tone was a little anxious now, thanks to her own uncertainties.

Amanda turned, lifting her shoulders in an expression of helpless understanding. "I know you do, darling. I know you do."

And they both tried to smile, just a little, but the effort fell flat in the silent kitchen. After a long moment, the older woman went back to poking the potatoes. "Dinner will be ready in a couple minutes. Think you can stay long enough to see your father?"

Grateful that her mother had changed tracks, Kassidy munched slowly on yet another doughnut as she wondered what had provoked her mother's disappointment. It couldn't be because her daughter was trying to get back together with Matt. Amanda Canyon had loved her son-in-law, and she still did. Logically she should have been delighted with Kassidy's planned reunion. Frustrated because she didn't understand and knew there was something she was overlooking in the overall scheme of things, Kassidy put the half-finished doughnut aside and checked the clock to see how long it would be before her father was due home. Another hour, she guessed, knowing she'd be right, give or take five minutes.

His schedule never varied, and she'd grown up knowing precisely when to expect him home, rain or shine. Kassidy's father had worked in the same hardware store all his life, content with the slow pace, the lack of change, earning a modest salary that almost kept up with a modest life-style. Kassidy had never understood his lack of ambition, particularly during those times when money had been scarce and unforeseen emergencies abounded. She hadn't really resented growing up in a household where money was a problem, but had never understood why her parents hadn't taken corrective measures. There were all sorts of things people could do to improve their financial status—better planning, better choices, and perhaps working more or even changing jobs.

No, Kassidy couldn't understand her parents at all. They'd been satisfied with things as they were, happy to have what they did, not worrying too much about the future. If it hadn't been for the retirement package included in her father's work benefits, they wouldn't have a dime outside of social security when he finally retired.

Kassidy had grown up wanting more for herself—not only material things. Security, financial security was her goal. Because of this, she knew she tended to be a little, well, miserly. This frugality was the complete antithesis of Matt's carefree spending habits.

"I asked if you were staying to dinner," her mother said from a point just behind her shoulder, the surprise intrusion into her thoughts a welcome respite. "Although how my pot roast can compete with those doughnuts, I'm sure I can't imagine."

Kassidy ignored the jibe and shrugged into her jacket. "Sorry, Mom. I need to get back to the office if I'm going to take any time off on Sunday." And she'd planned to take several hours off, sharing them with Matt as they celebrated their new commitment. Positive thinking, she reminded herself as she kissed her mother and followed her to the front door.

"It seems to me that a job that needs that many hours of your time is too demanding."

"The job's okay, Mom," Kassidy insisted. "But if I want to be the best, I have to try harder."

"Is being the best that important, Kassidy?" Amanda asked her daughter as they walked arm in arm down the steps to the sidewalk.

"Of course it is!" Surprised that she'd needed to ask, Kassidy kissed her on the cheek and pulled open the door of her car. "I can't imagine settling for anything less." She was bewildered by the sadness she noticed in Amanda Canyon's eyes. Being the best...making the big bucks...it had always been her goal.

"Being the best isn't good enough if you're alone, dear," the older woman murmured before turning away.

Kassidy sighed impatiently, slamming the door hard as she shoved the key into the ignition. Why couldn't everyone accept that you could have it all? Work, marriage, family...happiness. There was room for it all—most of the time, anyway. And when the demands of work took precedence over other responsibilities...well, everyone had to make choices, Kassidy told herself. It wasn't as though she didn't have time for other things, too. In fact, she could count on being busy twenty-four hours a day.

Matt should fit into her schedule just fine, Kassidy decided. It would work this time; she'd make it work. And if she tried really hard, she wouldn't have to give up anything else...except, perhaps, a little sleep. Humming in harmony with the tune on the radio, Kassidy set a course for the office. She figured she had an hour to work before meeting the girls of her Scout troop. They were baking muffins tonight, she recalled, wondering if Millie had done the shopping. Reaching into the console, she picked up her phone to call. If Millie had forgotten, Kassidy figured she could squeeze in a trip to the store.

There was time for everything, she thought with satisfaction as she waited for her call to be answered. All you needed was a little organization, and you could do it all.

6

KASSIDY STARED HARD at the man standing behind first base. Squinting into the harsh rays of the afternoon sun, her greedy eyes absorbed as many details as possible from her seat on the bleachers. His tan had deepened, she noticed.

And over the last hour or so, his scowl had lightened considerably. At least, she told herself it had. It was really hard to tell from this distance, but Kassidy wasn't tempted to get any closer, not for the time being anyway.

Maybe later, when he saw the humor in it all, he'd be a little more approachable.

Then again, perhaps not.

Kassidy winced as she recalled his exact words. "Wherever did you get the idea that I would appreciate having my sex life paraded the length and breadth of Puget Sound?" he'd stormed in the privacy of the empty dugout. "I've been back from camping three hours, and seven people have called about one thing or the other, and all they wanted to know was whether or not I was sleeping with my ex-wife! Seven people!" he'd shouted, holding up the same number of fingers just inches from her nose.

"Perhaps I'll come back later," Kassidy had muttered under her breath, looking past his shoulder toward the only escape from the half-buried dugout. "When you're feeling a little more rational."

"More rational!" he'd thundered, towering over her in the semidarkness of the structure. "What makes you think I'll ever be more rational?"

"It's not as bad as it sounds," Kassidy had suggested, realizing too late that meeting Matt alone—before everyone else showed up for the game—hadn't been her best strategy. "If you hadn't snuck out of the hotel before I woke up—"

"I didn't sneak out!" he'd sputtered, turning on his heel to pace the short distance to the door. "I tried to wake you, but all I got was moans and groans."

"And you think that was *my* fault?" More at ease now that they were back at the crux of the matter, Kassidy had tracked Matt to the end of the dugout, hands on hips and spitting mad. "You keep me awake all night . . . not just part of it, but *all* of it, and expect me to roll out with the birds?" Getting into the rhythm as her blood warmed to the argument, she'd thrown her best shot. "And it wasn't as though I called around to advertise. I was merely looking for you, so we could talk about it! I guess I happened to mention you'd left, without telling me where you were going." It was a little lie, but perhaps enough to get her off the hook.

Obviously, Matt hadn't agreed. "Talk about what?" he'd shouted, marching her backward to the opposite end of the dugout until her back was hard against the cold concrete block. Imprisoning her with his hands flat on the wall beside her head, he'd bowed his head until only a breath kept them apart. And then, so softly that she'd shivered, he'd asked her again, "Talk about what, Kassidy?"

"About what we're going to do about us," she'd whispered, a little afraid now that she'd pushed him too far . . . silently praying she'd pushed him far enough. Staring up into eyes that had never been anything but warm and caring, Kassidy wondered if this was the same man she'd married and divorced. His eyes were burning, the rich, sherry brown now blazing with a fire she'd never known.

Such emotion, such anger had never been evident in Matt before, not even at the height of their worst arguments.

This man, this new Matt, was as unexpected as he was appealing, and Kassidy had found herself beguiled by the change—beguiled and incredibly exhilarated. "I don't know if you're really mad or just taking this as an excuse to argue."

"I don't need an excuse to argue with you," he'd said, his eyes glued to the sudden promise in hers. "We did it all the time we were married."

"Not like this," she'd returned, her lips almost touching his as the words floated between them. "I don't remember ever arguing like this."

"I guess you've never done anything this stupid," he'd commented, eyes narrowing as he watched her. Then he'd frowned.

"Are you going to be mad for long?"

"I'm not sure yet," he'd said and scowled. "It might be smart if you'd keep your distance for a while, though."

"How long is a while?" she'd whispered, searching his face for a softening behind the harsh glare. It hadn't been there, but she wasn't particularly worried. It had been in his voice.

"I'll let you know."

MATT CAREFULLY AVOIDED looking toward the bleachers. It was easier to keep the scowl on his face if he didn't look at her, but at the rate things were moving, he didn't figure he'd last more than another hour, max.

He had been shocked to return from camping to find the gossip mill abuzz with her plotting. Because that was what it was, pure and simple. Kassidy, in her typical bulldozer fashion, had decided upon a goal and had proceeded to attain it.

It had been a shock, because he'd expected a wholly different gamut of emotions from his ex-wife, none of which was remotely associated with the almost wicked tactics of her smear campaign.

He grinned, turning from the bleachers to hide his mirth from Kassidy as he recalled the chortling glee with which Charlie had imparted the news. And Jack had called to spout some similar nonsense about the propriety of sending wedding gifts to a couple embarking upon another try at marriage—in a word, he refused to be fleeced a second time.

If making himself unavailable to Kassidy for a week had been designed to provoke a reaction from her, then he'd succeeded. Wondering if there was anything else up her sleeve to worry about, he finally forgave himself for the cat ploy—even if it had been Amanda's idea. The guilt he'd incurred by driving her from her own home was now expiated in full. Matt coughed a couple of times to override his chuckles before he turned back to the game, his attention anywhere but on the players.

The easy part was over. They were—or would be, after some minor maneuvering—on the verge of a new beginning. Tomorrow he'd discover if she was serious enough to tackle the hard part.

"I PROMISED THE BOYS miniature golf and burgers."

Kassidy grabbed his arm as he turned to follow the team to the parking lot. She couldn't believe it, simply couldn't believe he wasn't ready to talk.

She'd been ready for an entire week.

"Does this mean you're still mad at me?" she inquired slowly. Two full games she'd sat there and waited for a sign to tell her everything was okay. Two interminable games without so much as a wave to let her know he remembered she was there.

And now he was leaving without her? Kassidy's mood of contrition disappeared, replaced by a temper so vicious that even she was surprised. Rarely did she allow herself to become overwrought, and never over something as unimportant as a scheduling problem.

Matt pretended to think about it, grinning when he saw what his delaying tactics had netted. Kassidy was so mad— or frustrated, he preferred to think—that he could practically see the smoke coming out of her ears. Turning his back on the boys, he lifted her chin with his forefinger and dragged his thumb along the line of her jaw. "All it means is I've promised the boys a treat and I can't back out of it. I'll see you tomorrow."

"Tomorrow?"

"Unless you can't fit me into your Sunday schedule?" he taunted, ignoring the sudden knotting of the muscles in his shoulders. This was one of the problems they needed to address—Kassidy's compulsive need to work weekends. But he couldn't hope for miracles, particularly when she wasn't even aware of the changes that needed to be made.

"You're too busy for me tonight, so I get to rearrange everything to see you tomorrow? Is that what you're saying?" Kassidy was at boiling point, an emotional teakettle set to pierce the air with a scream and a hiss.

"I made this commitment last week, before the dance, before I let you seduce me," he said quietly, teasing her with his words as his fingers held her chin firm. "If I'd known how complicated things were going to get, I would have done things differently."

Kassidy stopped herself from biting back in the nick of time. There was something familiar about what he was saying, the way he was saying it . . . something sincere. Her next breath was held tight in her chest as she searched his face for a sign of what had changed in the last few moments. Her gaze sought his, looking, remembering. And then she knew.

It was the same gentle, pigheaded sweetness she'd fallen in love with.

Kassidy felt her pent-up breath drift between her lips in a sigh as her anger faded into oblivion. This Matt, the one whose soft, sherry eyes could melt her heart...this Matt was the man she loved.

The fingers at her chin fell away as he measured her lack of resistance, and before she could fathom what he was about, he dipped his head to plant a warm, hard kiss on her lips.

Kassidy had just begun to realize what was happening when it was over, and he was talking again.

"I'll call you tomorrow," he said softly, backing away a few steps before turning to jog through the parking lot toward the loaded vans.

Kassidy watched him go. And when the dust had settled in the wake of the vans, she meandered over to her car. Tomorrow, she thought, giving his suggestion due consideration.

"Well, hell," she muttered aloud, "tomorrow just won't do. It's tonight or nothing." That decision made, Kassidy was trying to determine whether she should go home or back to the office for the intervening hours when she was overwhelmed by an unaccustomed urge to go shopping. Looking at her watch, and calculating when she could expect Matt to be finished with the boys, Kassidy threw her purse onto the floor behind the front seat and revved the motor. The mall was only a few miles away, but she was suddenly anxious to get there. Throwing the car into gear, she whipped into traffic, accelerated across the intersection, then turned right to follow the access road to the freeway.

KASSIDY SHIFTED her weight from one foot to the other, listening hard for sounds of life behind the door. There weren't any, so she punched the bell again, this time holding it longer.

He still didn't come.

Checking her watch, she stifled her impatience with rare success and considered her options. One, she could turn around and go home. Wrinkling her nose in disgust at the thought of giving up so easily, she considered option number two, sitting on the front steps until Matt returned.

No thanks, she decided. There were better places to wait, like inside the house. Digging into her purse for her key ring, she selected the one she'd never imagined using again and inserted it into the lock. Moving quickly before she lost her nerve, Kassidy stepped inside and shut the door behind her.

"And that, Beethoven, is what keys are for," she said into the silence as the bust of the great musician glared at her from its perch atop the bookshelves that ran along the far wall. Kassidy stuck out her tongue at the bust, feeling no qualms about interacting with a lifeless object. After all, there was no one here to notice the trivial eccentricity.

"I know you never liked ol' Beethoven there, but do you have to abuse him?"

Kassidy reacted swiftly, biting her tongue in surprise. "Ouch, dammit!" she yelped, slurring the words as her tongue hesitated to perform.

"Outh dammith?" Matt inquired, totally incapable of hiding the smirk behind an innocent expression of concern.

Kassidy shot him a quick scowl before crossing to the beveled mirror above the bookcases, taking care to step over a baseball mitt and bat that he'd left in the middle of the floor. Carefully tweaking her tongue between thumb and forefinger, she pulled it out to check for damage.

"Let me see," Matt offered, strolling across the hall to stare with genuine concern at the wounded speech organ. "I've had a lot of experience with tongues."

Kassidy eyed him forbiddingly. "Touch my tongue and I'll have your fingers for supper!" she threatened, trying to keep a grin from escaping. Matt was back from playing with the boys, and she wouldn't have to wait until tomorrow to find out if he was interested in her proposition.

"I wasn't intending to use my fingers," he murmured, his gaze drifting over the picture they made within the mirror's frame. It was not unlike several others they'd had taken over the brief span of their marriage, each looking straight into the camera's lens, Kassidy's ebony curls contrasting with his blond waves. Matt wished he could frame the image now, catch that look of wary anticipation that heated her gaze.

Kassidy blushed at the deeply sensual note in his voice, not having the least doubt as to the kind of proposition he had in mind. His eyes were bright with laughter he couldn't hide. She turned away, fighting the need to snuggle up to his warm body and give in to the sexual cravings he'd awakened within her.

There was business to discuss.

"I rang the bell," she said, walking over to retrieve her purse, which she'd dropped. "Twice."

"I never imagined that you hadn't," he returned, following closely as she led the way down the hall into the kitchen. "I was out back. Besides, I thought we'd decided to wait until tomorrow."

"No, *we* didn't." Climbing onto her favorite stool, Kassidy faced Matt across the counter in the dwindling light.

"You suggested tomorrow. I didn't agree to anything of the sort."

She waited, suppressing her own impatience as Matt considered her words. She watched as he moved slowly around the kitchen, flicking on the overhead light, organizing the ingredients for hot chocolate with frequent glances in her direction. He was a little off balance, she thought, his frankly inquisitive gaze lingering on her for long moments between preparations.

What could he possibly be curious about? she wondered. Was there any doubt in his mind as to why she was there? How could he not know what she'd come prepared to propose...or why she couldn't wait until tomorrow? Too full of questions without answers, Kassidy distracted herself by staring at the assorted piles of junk on the various countertops. One looked as though it were mail and old newspapers mixed together, while another might have been outgoing letters—bills, probably—along with something that looked like diagrams of football plays. The rest of the kitchen was just as messy, with a stack of dishes drying beside the sink and miscellaneous pots and pans scattered about, waiting to be put away.

Matt had *always* been a slob, she remembered. Grimacing at the prospect of living with that again, Kassidy sternly told herself that neatness didn't count for everything, and maybe she'd be more tolerant this time around.

She was beginning to realize that not everything was going to be easy.

She watched the play of muscles across Matt's shoulders as he poured the steaming chocolate into mugs. The knit shirt he wore pulled tautly over his rippling shoulders, emphasizing his flowing strength and ease with the simple task. It reminded her of other activities, ones that took real strength, when those same muscles strained and pulled. She had never ceased to love watching Matt at play, throwing the football, backhanding a racket, springing across a field of grass.

Kassidy thought, too, of those times when he'd gathered her into his arms, giving her the chance to feel firsthand the strength that was so much a part of him. She shut her eyes against the sensual greed of her body as memories full of elementary needs stroked already sensitized nerves. She felt the tightening of her nipples beneath the silk camisole . . . almost moaned aloud at the incredibly erotic sensations. Just one of her purchases from that afternoon's shopping spree, the camisole slipped and slithered against her body with the slightest breath. The peach-toned, cotton sweater she'd pulled over it provided a secondary excitement, its delicate ribbing dragging lightly over the tight buds, slipping easily across the silk at her every movement.

She wondered how it would feel to have Matt's hands sliding across the silken camisole, the heat of his palms adding to the friction. She was so involved with the impromptu fantasy that when he spoke, she jumped in surprise, her eyes flying open as she registered his nearness.

"If you came to seduce me again, you're doing a pretty good job of it."

The husky timbre of his voice calmed her jangled nerves, soothed her with the promise of more talk, more love. He was just across the counter, the mugs of chocolate gripped tightly in hands that almost appeared to shake. Kassidy was startled at the intensity of need that burned in his eyes, felt her lips part in an invitation that she couldn't leash.

"Is that why you came, Kassidy?" he asked softly, lowering his forearms until the mugs rested on the counter. "You want to make love with me . . . to me?"

Kassidy gulped, the lump in her throat making it almost impossible to swallow. Making love sounded good, she thought, better than the talk she'd intended to have with him. Another chance to show him with her body how well suited they were, one more opportunity to immerse herself in the high-flying thrills of Matt's loving caresses.

Her fingers tightened over the edge of the counter, the simmering heat of her excitement making her grasp a little slippery, her fingers less than steady. Holding Matt's searching gaze with her own, she tried for an answer that wouldn't sound crassly lecherous.

"It was certainly a featured segment in my plans tonight," she said slowly, smiling at her own thoughts before seeing something dark and fiery shoot through his eyes. It was there, and then it wasn't. She plunged ahead, wondering what he was hiding . . . and why she was more nervous than before. "I had really thought to propose marriage to you first," she said, "but I can always do that later."

"Marriage?" Matt quirked one eyebrow in Kassidy's direction, as though it were a foreign word. Beyond that single, controlled reaction, he managed to maintain an air of vague curiosity. "Now that's an interesting concept." Shoving a mug of chocolate across the counter, he lifted the other and sipped thoughtfully.

"It's not exactly an inconceivable notion," Kassidy returned warily, gulping the hot liquid in search of its more soothing qualities. Burning her tongue instead, she smacked the cup back onto the counter and nursed her scalded tongue for a second or two before taking up her train of thought once more. "I just figured we were in a position to give it another try." *Not to mention that I've never stopped loving you,* she said into the silent void between them.

Matt lowered his eyelids against her stare, hiding the relief he felt at her proposal . . . and the uneasiness over her too simplistic view of the situation. *Had she even bothered to think beyond the passion?*

"So one night of sex, and you're ready to jump back into that hellhole we called a marriage—"

"It's more than sex."

"Probably," he granted, tossing back the last of his chocolate before turning away to the sink where he carefully rinsed the dark sediment from the bottom of the cup. He took his time, going over in his mind the words he'd rehearsed a hundred times. But when he faced her, it was as though he'd never anticipated what he would say to her if they ever got this far.

At this point they had a fantasy in the making. Now they just had to make it work.

"It probably *was* more than sex," he continued, as though trying to be fair. "But not enough. We had all that and more when we were married, and where did it leave us?" Feigning indifference, he crossed his arms over his chest and leaned back against the sink, watching her from across the room as she struggled with her arguments. She looked beautiful tonight, more so than he remembered. The soft peach of her sweater made her skin appear almost translucent, the shiny, black curls falling in sexy disorder about her face, the trembling of the wide, sensuous mouth. He grimaced a little as he noted the shockingly tight jeans that smoothed over her legs, coating her hips and fanny almost like a second skin. He shot that image into the far corners of his mind, to a place where all the other sensual thoughts were awaiting their turn. A place where, just moments ago, he'd thrown his awareness of her tightening nipples, pushing out under her thin sweater in outrageous temptation.

"Are you saying you don't want to give us another try?" she finally asked, dumbfounded that she could have been so wrong about everything. But she must have been, she realized. Matt didn't look the least bit thrilled by her proposal. In fact he appeared barely curious, almost dispassionately so.

"I haven't said anything one way or the other," he returned, shrugging as though the conversation were a mite boring. "I'm just trying to find out if you know what you're after."

"You!" she exploded, leaping off the stool. "I came over here to tell you I want to get married again!" Kassidy slammed the flat of her palm onto the counter, keeping the barrier of the counter between them as her passion exploded into unfamiliar rage. *"I love you and I want to marry you. . . . And all you can do is stare at me and act as though we're talking about what movie we should see!"*

It took everything he had to restrain himself. "I love you, too," he said. "That's never changed. Unfortunately, that's not all that hasn't changed."

"What are you talking about?" she demanded.

"You. Me. All the things we did to make each other crazy," he said, his voice clipped as though he were reciting from a list. "Nothing's changed. Getting married again under those circumstances would be disastrous."

Kassidy heard what he was saying, but refused to understand. She didn't *want* to understand, because that would mean her dreams were disappearing before her eyes. "We could try harder—"

"At what?" he scoffed. "Ignoring what's wrong? No, Kassidy, it won't work."

He'd finally gotten through to her, Matt realized, as he watched the first hint of tears welling at her lashes, the unnatural brightness of her sapphire eyes as she fought the uncharacteristic lapse. The tears decided him, the subtle shaking of her shoulders brought him around the counter until there were just inches between them. Lifting a hand that was trembling with an emotion he couldn't control, he ran a finger under her eyes, allowing the tears to spill onto his fingertips. Again and again he cleansed her with his callused fingers as she watched, bemused and suddenly calm.

"Quite a dilemma, isn't it, love?" Matt asked softly.

"I guess that's that, then," she said, taking a deep breath for strength and easing back just a few inches so that when she, too, raised her fingers to her eyes, she wouldn't have to touch him. Touching him now was too familiar a gesture. . . . "I'll just get out of your way."

"You give up too easily," he chided, a little disappointed, but relieved to see her eyes clearing. "That's what happened the first time around, love. We both gave up too easily."

"Dammit, Matt! I feel like I'm running in circles!" Quelling the impulse to stomp down the hall and slam the front door behind her, she glared belligerently at the man who was confusing her so thoroughly. "First you tell me it's not a good plan, then you call me a quitter when I try to walk away. Is this some kind of game to make me crazy?" she shouted, her chest heaving with the adrenaline rush of a new battle. "What do you want me to do?"

"Change."

She gasped. "Change?" The word seemed to leave a foreign taste on her lips as she stared up at him, bewildered and a little afraid.

"Change," he said again, stepping back in his turn so that they could talk without touching. "Not just you, Kassidy. Me, too. It's not enough that we love each other. We've got to learn to live together if we're going to have any chance at all."

"I have to *change?*" she asked, shaking her head abruptly as she tried to clear her head of the conflicting waves of thought. "If I want you, I have to change?"

He nodded slowly. "And compromise," he added. "Give a little, take a little. We never did that before. If you want us to stop the fighting, it's the only answer," he said carefully.

"I can do that," she replied quickly, her spirits lifting, because there was finally something concrete she could deal with, and because it didn't sound as if he was saying no any longer. "Just tell me what I have to do." After all, she could do anything she set her mind to. That was why being blessed with a Type-A personality was so handy—achieving one's goals was simply a matter of hard work and determination.

He shook his head. "No, Kassidy. *You* tell *me*."

An added degree of difficulty. Kassidy backed up a little, both figuratively and physically, until she was sitting on the stool again. "You want little things or big things?"

"Both."

Kassidy looked at him carefully, watched as he bowed his head so that his eyes were trained on the idle movement of his fingers on the cool tiles of the counter. It dawned on her, then, that Matt had given more thought to their reunion than she'd supposed . . . much more thought than Kassidy herself had given it. Where she'd kept her hopes pinned on their continued love, their sexual compatibility, Matt had dug deeper into the shaky foundations of their marriage.

All of a sudden her heart skipped a beat as she realized the enormity of what needed to be done to cement the relationship between them. A shiver of fear tickled her spine, and she wondered if she had the strength to do her part.

Lifting his gaze to hold hers, he challenged her to take the ultimate test. "It won't be enough to modify a few quirks," he said. "We'll have to compromise on some pretty major things here."

"Like work?" she asked, knowing her chances were one in a million he'd say no.

He didn't.

"That's one," Matt agreed, nodding solemnly. "I won't marry Superwoman, not again."

"I don't understand," Kassidy fibbed, knowing exactly what he was getting at. She just didn't want to talk about it. "You're the superhero. I'm just a run-of-the-mill stock-broker."

"Not run-of-the-mill," he objected. "You're the best you can be . . . better than anyone else."

"You don't want me to be the best?"

"I want you to be happy," he countered, "for *us* to be happy. And I know that your spending every waking moment working isn't doing it."

"Not every moment," she returned, skipping over the part about happiness; she didn't want to think about how happy or successful she might be giving up the habits of a lifetime. "I always made time for other things."

"Like the Girl Scouts. And story hour, to mention a couple."

"You want me to give up Girl Scouts?" she asked, puzzled; he'd always encouraged her work with the young girls.

Matt shook his head slowly, pleased with Kassidy's response. The negotiations had begun, and she hadn't rejected the idea out of hand, not yet.

Matt leaned against the refrigerator door and continued. "It was never a problem of how much you managed to pack into your day—more a matter of wondering where I fit into it. Or if someday it might become too inconvenient to spare me any time at all."

"I wanted to get ahead," she said, then fell silent as he held up a hand in protest.

"I can't argue with that, but I always felt your job was more important than our marriage." And then, before she had a chance to reply, he added, "I know the future is important to you, that security is important. But I never knew if you'd ever get to that magical point where enough was enough."

"The harder I work, the faster I'll reach that point," she argued.

"And how will you know when you get there?"

She didn't have an answer for that. It had never occurred to her that someday there might be a point when she wouldn't have to worry anymore. No, she decided, that wasn't something she was prepared to talk about. Not tonight.

Sidestepping his question, she inquired, "You want me to work less?"

Matt rephrased his query. "I think you need to ease up a little."

"How much is a little?"

"You might consider working the same hours as your associates, more or less," he said, holding his breath. Would she fly off the handle at this presumptuous suggestion?

She did.

"But most of them leave by two or three o'clock, four at the latest!" she exclaimed. "And they hardly ever come in on weekends!" Being a stockbroker on this coast might be considered grueling timewise, especially if one wasn't a morning person, because the market opened at six-thirty—nine-thirty in New York—which meant one had to be in the office by five-thirty or six to get organized. But with the market closing at one o'clock, early afternoons were the payoff in Seattle—a phenomenon she'd never experienced.

"And do they get fired for that?" he asked, as though genuinely curious. He knew the answer. So did she. It was just time for her to admit it.

"No, but—"

"It's only a suggestion," he said gently. "I can't make you do anything you don't want to do."

Kassidy looked at him for a long moment without replying. "What do I get?" she finally asked.

"Excuse me?" Matt was having a little trouble keeping up; he'd expected her to continue arguing.

"If I give up working so hard, where is the compromise?" she wanted to know, determined to get her pound of flesh out of the bargain. "It's not like I can ask you to work less! You're the one who knows all about making work a sixth priority."

"Suppose I offer to work more? Would that satisfy you?"

The knowledge of how far he was willing to go hit her hard. Matt, the consummate sportsman, was willing to work. Shaking her head in stunned disbelief, she felt the tension between them begin to dissipate. But before she could reply, he added more.

"Money," he said. "Our spending habits are totally opposed."

"Kind of like our saving habits," she added dryly.

Matt nodded in agreement. "I'm not saying it will be easy, but we should be able to sit down like two adults and discuss it."

"That'll be the day," Kassidy said, not quite under her breath, and was surprised when Matt almost pinned her to the floor with a stern look that chastised her for such levity.

"We can't just pretend it's not a problem," he reminded her. "If we ignore it, it won't just disappear. That's what this is all about."

"You really think we can resolve our differences?" she asked.

"I think we can try."

And he believed it, she realized, feeling the strength of his determination flow into her. Just to test the waters, she plunged in. "Food," she said succinctly. "The stuff you eat—"

"Will enable me to live a long and healthy life," he finished, referring to his normal diet. "On the other hand, your eating habits are the stuff of which nightmares are made. Between the leftovers you cart home from all those business lunches—"

"Nothing like a free meal," she snapped, recollecting without any difficulty his disgust at the doggie bags she'd almost daily thrown into the refrigerator.

"And all that fast food!" Matt shuddered, still as appalled by her devotion to tacos, burgers and pizza as he'd been by her insistence that there was a form of nutrition in each item. The lowest form, he figured, wondering about her cholesterol level and if she'd ever gotten around to having it checked.

"I love fast food. You knew that when I married you," she insisted, remembering the nights they'd made do with a burger picked up at the local drive-thru.

"I thought it was a phase," he said and smiled, remembering the highly salted junk food he'd ingested in those moments they'd remembered there was more to life than sex. There hadn't been time for more, he'd thought, figuring it was more a matter of convenience than want when she'd repeatedly pulled into the drive-thru.

He'd been wrong, of course. Fast food was one of the mainstays of her life. Matt wondered for a moment what kind of compromise they could make, if they'd ever be able to eat a meal together.

It was worth a moment's hesitation.

"You're a slob," she suddenly said, bringing up another of the sources of their daily battles.

But Matt just nodded slowly as though agreeing with her, and went on to another point. "What about books?"

Kassidy winced. He would have to bring that up! Trying to read any of Matt's books used to drive her over the edge, not to mention the tense moments when he found the results of her foray into his section of the library. While Kassidy firmly believed that all books needed to have their spines cracked in order to render them readable, Matt refused to allow the practice on his own property. Everything from paperbacks to hard covers was out-of-bounds to her mutilating hands, making reading any of his books an excruciating experience. At first Kassidy had attempted caution, turning each page until the book was barely cracked open, peering down into the well of words that flowed into the shadows and onto the following page.

In frustration, she'd finally given up. She'd gone ahead and read the books in the manner to which she was accustomed, breaking their backs and returning them to the shelf when she was done, hoping without much conviction that he wouldn't notice.

He'd noticed.

"I don't have an answer for that," she said, this apparently trivial point bringing home the sheer hopelessness of their quest. She'd never be able to read a book without cracking its back. Some habits were impossible to break.

Matt seemed not to expect to hear anything different.

"We never learned to live together," he finally said, drawing her gaze into the depth of his own. "We never tried."

"We tried . . ."

"No, Kassidy. We didn't. We never learned the meaning of compromise, never attempted to minimize the damage of all those arguments. We were too . . . too stubborn."

His analysis of the failure of their marriage stopped her. And frightened her, because she didn't know if there was a better way.

"So you're saying we're a hopeless case?" she asked softly, her palm caressing the smooth tile of the countertop.

"I'm saying we need to go into this with our eyes open," he said, surprising her with a renewed note of hope. "We have to confront the problems, talk about them, learn to change. Both of us. That's the only way it's going to work."

Matt bowed his head to study the pattern of the floor tiles, mulling over the last of what he would say to her. It was important that she understand this was their only chance. If they blew things this time, there would be nothing left upon which to build.

"Détente," he said softly, looking up to catch the grin on Kassidy's face as she connected the global concept with their infinitely smaller alliance. "I figure if we work real hard, we too can accomplish a major cessation of hostilities."

"Isn't that a little presumptuous?" she asked, enjoying the way his lips formed the word. *Détente*, she repeated silently. What a unique approach to a tiny conflict.

"It worked for the bear and the eagle," he offered. "I figured we might give it a try."

"Why does that sound like it came over the loudspeaker at a ball game?" she chided him. She enjoyed his chortle of laughter and luxuriated in the warmth of his approval. *Détente*. Kassidy tried the word again, found herself intrigued by it.

"And if it doesn't work?" she asked, suddenly afraid of a future without him. It was entirely possible she'd never be able to make the changes that would make him happy.

"Then we won't have made the same mistake twice." Crossing the few feet of kitchen that separated them, Matt lifted his hands until they were a warm friction on her arms. "Marriage, my love, will have to wait this time. But I want you here, in the house we bought together. It's the only way we'll be able to put this to the test."

"You want to *live* with me?" she squeaked, shivering in helpless response to the slow massage of his hands.

"For now," he agreed, sliding his palms across her shoulders to cup her chin. "For now, I suppose it's the best we can do."

And as he lowered his mouth to hers, Kassidy echoed his sentiments. "For now," she agreed.

Tomorrow, she figured, was another matter altogether. Tomorrow she intended to prove to Matt just how much she could change. Or compromise, she amended, mentally squashing the budding unease that threatened to undermine her determination. She could do anything she set her mind to, she forcibly reminded herself as she opened her mouth to the wet thrust of his tongue.

Tofu couldn't possibly taste as bad as it looked.

7

"WHAT DID MARLA THINK about losing a roommate?"

Kassidy stowed the last load of clothes in the bottom drawer and kicked it shut with her toe before crossing to Matt's dresser to stuff inside a sock that dangled over the edge. "Personally, I think she was ecstatic, but she had the good taste not to show it."

"Outside of opening that bottle of champagne, you mean?" Rolling onto his feet from the low chair he'd fallen into as he'd watched Kassidy transfer her clothes from the cardboard boxes into the dresser and closet, Matt stretched, pushing his hands flat against the bedroom ceiling.

"I prefer to believe she intended that as an observance of our new status," Kassidy returned, giving her erstwhile roommate the benefit of the doubt. "Besides, things aren't going to change that much for her. I'm going to keep the condo, and she's going to stay there. The only difference is, she won't see me as often."

"I suppose you're right, considering how little time you spent there," he couldn't resist observing.

"I told you I was going to work on that," she said, refusing to be tricked into another debate on her schedule. Late last night they'd come to an agreement of sorts on that subject: Kassidy would make an effort to leave the office by midafternoon, most days. Considering the market closed on the West Coast at one o'clock, that would give her plenty of time to finish up any odds and ends she hadn't had time for during trading hours.

More to the point, she was going to try. It had sounded almost easy last night, lying in Matt's arms as they made plans together, each of them eager to prove they could accomplish the impossible with mere determination. Quelling her "light of day" doubts because she didn't want to think about them, she repeated her resolution to try. "I'm really going to work on it."

"Working on not working isn't precisely what I had in mind," Matt pointed out, deftly avoiding the swat she aimed at his butt as he crossed in front of her to look into the closet. On one side were his clothes. Most of them were hanging up, except for those he'd tossed across the lower rail, thinking he might wear them again but hadn't, because they'd gotten wrinkled as the pile grew. On the floor was a jumbled pile of shoes.

On the other side of the closet were Kassidy's things, her clothes a study in neatness, most of them still in the plastic bags that protected them from dust and wrinkles, her shoes in a neat row beneath. His shoes would look like that, too, if he'd just moved in, he consoled himself.

Kassidy went up on tiptoe to look over his shoulder, then gave him a look that fully expressed her disgust. But she didn't say anything, because it was their first day of living together, and she really couldn't expect him to change overnight.

Matt flicked off the light and backed out of the closet, trying not to laugh aloud as Kassidy, attempting to do the same, almost tripped over one of the many boxes that were strewn about the room. "I'll get these boxes down to the garage while you start working on the library," he offered.

"Have you dusted in there this year?" she asked, not looking forward to the inch of allergy-tormenting dust she was sure to find.

"I had a cleaning service go through the place last month," he said gruffly, as though the character assassination was misplaced.

"Those people cost a fortune!" she exclaimed. "Don't you realize how much you could save—?"

The telephone rang, saving Matt from a little lecture. Trying to keep the worry from showing on his face, he decided to put off telling her about the maid he planned to hire next week. The decision was a compromise, he persuaded himself, swallowing hard as he wondered how he'd explain things to Kassidy. Not only did hiring a maid allow him to continue being a slob, but her wages were also money Kassidy wouldn't have spent. Wrong on two counts, she was going to say.

Maybe he'd wait two weeks before telling her.

Kassidy shot him a look of sheer exasperation, then jumped over a box to pick up the ringing phone. It was one of her Scouts. "Hi, Nicole! How'd you find me so quick?"

"Your roommate said you moved. She said you were living in Coach Hill's house," the youngster went on, making the move sound like the most exciting thing that had happened since Mt. St. Helens blew.

Wishing Marla had stopped with the number when giving information, Kassidy gulped; she really hadn't thought about how she was going to explain this to the girls. Since lying wouldn't get her anywhere, she tried for a bald statement of truth. "That's right, Nicole. I've moved in with my ex-husband."

The basic facts obviously weren't enough for the precocious youngster on the other end of the line. "Is it okay to tell my mom and dad you're living with a guy, then?"

"He's not 'a guy,' he's my ex-husband," Kassidy corrected, shrugging her shoulders at Matt's raised eyebrows.

"And of course it's okay, Nicole. Just tell them I've moved in with him because we want to try it again."

"Try what again?"

Even Kassidy knew when she was being teased, so she put an end to the questions before they got even more personal. "What can I do for you, Nicole? Are you calling about the cookies?"

Nicole appeared to take the hint and embarked on a long tale that had something to do with Nancy's violin practice. Since she couldn't help bake cookies on Tuesday, her mom wouldn't be driving the car pool, and that left three of the other girls without a ride. Kassidy stretched across the bed to grab her purse and was looking through it for her personal phone book when Matt left the room with the first load of boxes. She told Nicole to call Mary's mom, because her van held six or seven, and to call back if that didn't work out.

By the time Matt returned for the second load, she'd obviously said goodbye to Nicole, and was deep in conversation with Millie about the possibility of changing the cookie-bake night to another if the car pool change didn't work out. Resisting the temptation to lie down beside her, Matt reminded himself he was due to tee up in half an hour and picked up another stack of boxes for the garage. Maybe by the time he'd played eighteen holes, Kassidy would be finished sorting out her things in the library.

Then again, perhaps he'd beg off after nine. Wearing a satisfied smile, Matt blindly negotiated the steps and headed for the garage.

IT WAS BARELY THREE O'CLOCK.

Kassidy congratulated herself as she nosed her car through a yellow light and flipped around the corner where the bank's time and temperature sign flashed the encouraging news that it was seventy-eight degrees, a sweltering day for early spring in the Northwest. Kassidy, however, was oblivious to this variation from the norm, having little or no experience at being out of the office at this time of day.

The temperature made her yearn for the soothing comfort of the pool. Making up her mind that she'd wallow in the heated waters the second she rid herself of the wool business suit, she sped along the last two blocks and slid her car into the driveway. Throwing open the car door, she grabbed her briefcase and purse, not forgetting the white bag that held her leftovers from lunch. Slamming the door shut with a swift kick, she rounded the rusty hood, patting it with a light touch that nonetheless left a film of dust on her palm.

A quick check of the garage showed her Matt wasn't yet home from work. She tried to feel guilty, but failed. After all, she'd been at work since dawn's early light, while Matt probably hadn't rolled into the office much before ten. That was what came of being a stockbroker on the West Coast, she rationalized. Her day was half over before normal people got started, leaving her free to enjoy the empty afternoons while others toiled away.

Just because today was practically the first time she'd taken advantage of the early schedule didn't mean she couldn't appreciate it, Kassidy told herself. Too bad Matt wasn't a stockbroker, she mused, laughing aloud at the incongruity of the thought. Matt? A stockbroker?

Her imagination didn't stretch that far.

On impulse she detoured past the pool, kneeling down to test the water. She grinned as her fingers delved into the comforting warmth, the temperature of the water easily in excess of the air around her. In other words, she decided as she straightened and flicked the drops from her fingertips, it was perfect—much better than when she'd tested it at the crack of dawn. Shivering at the memory of the icy water, Kassidy congratulated herself on the foresight that had driven her to check the thermostat. Fifty-five degrees! "What nonsense!" she'd exclaimed in the still morning, flicking the tiny marker as far to the right as it would move.

Now, of course, the water was perfect. Eighty degrees, if the thermostat was to be believed. Kassidy dashed into the house, tossed her doggie bag into the refrigerator, dropped her briefcase onto a chair in the hallway and made a bee-line for the bedroom. She quickly changed into her bikini, ignoring the miscellaneous clothes Matt had tossed around the room—she wasn't in the mood to notice them—stopping only to make the bed because she hated sleeping in wrinkled sheets. It was Matt's job to make the bed during the week, they'd agreed, because Kassidy was up at about five and out of the house before Matt even opened his eyes. Maybe he'd take the hint when he saw she'd taken care of it herself, she hoped, pulling the last wrinkles from the spread before racing out of the room. In the garage she sifted through a box of pool accessories until she found an old air mattress. Taking down Matt's air pump from its hook on the wall, she impatiently filled the plastic with air.

And then, with care not to get her hair wet, she eased herself onto the raft and drifted into the center of the pool, her feet dangling off the side of the floating mattress.

The water, she decided, was as close to perfection as was possible outdoors. What would be the chances she could talk Matt into enclosing the pool? she wondered, picturing herself basking in the warm steam during a winter storm. The idea appealed, although the probable cost of such a venture appalled her.

Kassidy let her arms fall into the water, making no attempt to guide the craft. Instead, with limbs submerged and mind adrift, she relaxed.

IT WAS, MATT DECIDED, one of the few times he could remember seeing Kassidy totally limp. Peering through the
kitchen window, he watched as the float bumped softly
against the side of the pool until her little finger reached out
to push against the slick tiles. She did it without opening her
eyes, clearly using minimum effort to accomplish maximum results.

Retreating from the window, he dashed to their room and
threw off his clothes, not minding where they landed. He
found his swimming trunks hanging over the bathtub fau-
cet, still wringing wet from his early-morning swim. Slipping the clammy nylon up his legs, Matt grabbed a towel,
then leaped over the pile of clothes before charging back
down the stairs. Once out the kitchen door, he dropped the
towel and took a running dive toward the pool.

He knew something was wrong the moment his body hit
the water, but the unnatural heat slowed his thinking. Matt
swam the entire length of the pool underwater before his
brain unfuzzed enough to pinpoint the abnormality.

His pool was a boiling caldron, fit only for tropical fish.

He surfaced near the sloping steps at the shallow end, just
a few feet from where Kassidy lolled. His body was in low
gear, the extraordinary heat slowing his reflexes as he
dragged himself out of the water to drop onto the rough
concrete surface.

"Welcome home, stranger," Kassidy drawled without
opening her eyes. With a slight flick of her fingers, she sent
a spray of water arching through the air in the direction of
the man she sensed lying dazed beside the pool. A single lap,
and he was practically unconscious. This certainly wasn't
the athlete she remembered, Kassidy mused. Then she gig-
gled, recalling the previous night's activities, which con-
ceivably might have put a damper on his energy levels.

"How can you stand that water?" he asked, basking in the already cooling air of the late afternoon. "Didn't it occur to you the thermostat is broken?"

"Broken?"

"As in out of whack. That water's practically boiling."

"Guess I didn't notice," she said, hiding her disappointment. Maybe she shouldn't have set it so high, she thought, trying to recall what they'd done about this problem before. Then she remembered, and wasn't encouraged by the memory. They'd had the pool built just a couple of months before the divorce, Matt insisting he needed the convenience of this at-home exercise opportunity, Kassidy losing her cool when the bill arrived. Until then she'd only used it a couple of times, mostly because the temperature recommended by the pool man was generally too low for her. After seeing the bill, she'd refused to use it at all.

Blaming her selective memory for allowing her to mess with the thermostat, Kassidy resolved to try for a compromise—about seventy-five degrees.

"How long do you think you'll stay in there?"

Kassidy lifted a forearm to a point in front of her face, then pinched the slightly red skin. "A while longer," she said, closing her eyes again. "I'm not done yet."

"I'd say you're this side of well-done," Matt muttered, wondering how she could stand the cloying heat. "I'm going to check that thermostat."

"I'll be out soon," Kassidy promised, wondering where she'd get the energy to lift herself from the float. After last night, Matt wasn't the only one incapable of swimming laps.

There was a brief silence, and Kassidy used the time well, creating a story that was nearly plausible. Tomorrow would be soon enough to confront the issue.

"Someone's moved the setting!" Matt wandered back from the tiny room where the heating mechanism was located. "There's nothing wrong with it at all."

So much for tomorrow! "Maybe the pool man changed it by mistake," Kassidy offered, figuring it was worth a try.

"Maybe," he said, shaking his head in disbelief. "But I just can't imagine how he'd do something that stupid. He knows I like the pool cold."

Kassidy gave up. "I surrender!" she exclaimed with a sigh, pushing away from the side of the pool with a well-placed kick so she could talk without having to look at his you-should-have-known-better expression. "It was like ice this morning, so I changed it and I'm sorry, but I really didn't have any idea you really wanted it that cold!" She took a quick breath and continued. "But you don't have to worry about it anymore, because I won't do it again."

"*You* changed it?"

"Isn't that what I just said?"

There was a silence as Matt thought about it. "How are you going to like swimming . . . or floating, I suppose . . . in cold water?"

"I'm not," she said honestly, paddling a little so she could see Matt. "But it's really your pool, and I don't care that much about swimming, or whatever."

Matt nodded as though he agreed, hiding the flicker of an idea behind what he hoped was a bland expression. "I appreciate that, Kassidy. Really I do."

And that, she decided, was that. Tomorrow, the bathtub! Feeling good about something, but not knowing exactly what, she grinned up at him. "Try not to get fat in the meantime," she advised. "I know how you count on your exercise!"

"Don't tease me, woman," he cautioned. "Not if you want to come out of there with dry hair!"

Kassidy decided on a quick change of subject. "I don't suppose now is a good time to talk about what we're going to have for supper?"

"Why don't you let me take care of that tonight?" he offered, his eyes sweeping the nearly naked length of the woman beneath him. The tiny scraps that were meant to pass for a bikini tantalized him with their ability to cover those places that had been open for his view just last night. His gaze heated as he saw her body respond to his stare, her firm nipples pushing into the fragile barrier of cloth that was less of a barrier than an enticement.

"On second thought, why don't you just climb out of that bathwater and come help me in the kitchen?" he suggested in a low murmur, envisioning at least three activities that had nothing whatsoever to do with the preparation of dinner.

Kassidy gulped, almost arching off the float as his rough, rumbly voice stroked the sensitive nerves of her spine. It was so wonderfully exciting, sharing this tempestuous need with the man she loved, hiding nothing from him...or from herself. She wanted Matt, needed him, and nothing else seemed to matter.

Not even the prospect of eating veggie-burgers for dinner.

Totally undisciplined to the erotic atmosphere between them, her stomach growled in protest as she thought of Matt's version of a satisfying meal. It caught her by surprise, taking the edge off the sensual byplay.

Even Matt was sidetracked by the resounding gurgles. "I suppose you're trying to convince me you'd rather eat than anything else," he teased, groaning a little as he leaned forward to anchor the float against the side of the pool.

Kassidy decided to let her conflicting needs fight it out, ignoring the hand Matt offered as she slipped off the air mattress and climbed the steps to the pool's edge. Keeping her distance from the temptation of his lean, tanned body, she picked up the towel Matt had dropped earlier and bent to dry her thighs and calves.

"Maybe we ought to have dinner out," she suggested, tossing him the towel. She'd even go along to that restaurant next door to the bakery where everything was "naturally produced, without additives, etc." Kassidy wasn't even sure what that meant, except that the bread would be full of little seeds and chewy enough to make her jaw think it was doing calisthenics. Anything was better than facing one of Matt's homemade concoctions on an empty stomach.

"You're not being open-minded about this, Kassidy," he chided, throwing the towel over his shoulder and snagging her hand in his. Leading her toward the house, he tried to take the fear out of the unknown. "You've never tried anything I've ever cooked," he began.

"That's because all I ever saw in the refrigerator was bean sprouts and yogurt. My imagination doesn't stretch to a satisfying meal with those ingredients."

"Health food is one thing," he said patiently. "I prefer to think I eat healthy food." Pushing her through the open Dutch doors with a firm pressure between her shoulder blades, he propelled her to the refrigerator.

"There's a difference?"

"Between health food and healthy food?" Matt shrugged as he opened the refrigerator door and leaned over Kassidy as they jointly viewed the contents. "I like to think so."

"Are you comparing radishes to carrots, or what?" she asked, puzzled by the distinction.

"Not really. It's more a case of eating a balanced diet, with an emphasis on foods that are inclined to make me a healthy person . . . as opposed to that junk you seem to live on."

"I don't eat like that all the time," she huffed, her eye caught by the containers of yogurt that took up most of one shelf. She studiously ignored the warmth of Matt's chest against her back. Her priorities were already decided—she wanted food. Immediately, if possible. The little white bag with the picture of a hungry dog on the side was right where she'd put it, and she considered the merits of sneaking it out of the fridge for a sustaining nibble. Unfortunately Matt was breathing down her neck.

Kassidy sighed, dismissing the potentially appeasing, congealed lemon chicken from her thoughts. "I eat cereal once in a while, too. They say it's part of a balanced diet."

"Fruit Puffs?" he derided, avoiding the foot she brought up to slam on his bare toes. "You call that cereal?"

"Advertisers don't lie," she returned. "Besides, I love them."

"That probably has more impact on you than their nutritional value," he mumbled, pulling out a pound of hamburger along with a tomato, head of lettuce and fresh cucumber. Nudging Kassidy away from the cool air, he elbowed the door shut and loaded the counter with his choices. "Now, this is what we're going to have for dinner."

"Raw hamburger?"

"Ground round," he corrected her. "And it's eighty-eight percent fat free. That makes a difference."

"I bet it'll taste like raw hamburger," she shot back, edging away from the counter. "But I'll never collect on that, because I'm not eating it."

Matt watched as his bikini-clad ex-wife steadily retreated from the kitchen, backing into a counter before correcting her trajectory and slipping away into the hallway. "You'll eat it," he called after her, thrusting aside the temptation to follow her. Dinner could wait, he wanted to believe. Even with her obvious hunger, Matt was confident he could convince her to eat later.

But then, perhaps by that time he'd be too exhausted to cook, and they'd end up ordering a pizza. Shuddering at the thought, Matt broke the seal on the hamburger and proceeded to make thick patties of the lean beef. It would serve her right if he did serve it raw, he considered. Kassidy really had the wrong idea about his cooking!

KASSIDY PULLED the raw cucumber from the sandwich with her fingertips, tucking it under the crisp leaves of lettuce at the side of her plate.

"What's wrong with the cucumber?"

Damn! Matt didn't miss a thing. First he'd taken offense when she'd pulled out the lettuce. Now he was complaining about the cucumber. Who did he think she was—Bugs Bunny?

"The sandwich is kind of thick," she mumbled, eyeing the four-inch-high layers with misgiving. "I'm just trying to scale it to my mouth."

"You're trying to avoid eating the veggies," he contended.

That, too, she admitted silently. Aloud, she protested. "Not at all. The tomato is still there," she pointed out, wondering how she'd manage to get rid of that with Matt just across the table. It was bad enough she had to eat the hamburger—broiled and bulging, encased in some sort of bun that looked as if it came from his favorite bakery.

"Didn't your mom ever make homemade hamburgers?" he asked as Kassidy continued to poke and prod her sandwich.

"Lots of times," Kassidy said, glaring at the sandwich on her plate. "These look just like them."

"But I thought you loved hamburgers," Matt said around a mouthful of sandwich.

"A hamburger is what you eat out of paper bags after waiting in line for at least five minutes with twenty-five other hungry people. This, on the other hand, is an enormous patty of half-cooked meat surrounded by a week's worth of vegetables," Kassidy insisted firmly.

"It's not half-cooked," Matt argued, finishing his first burger and reaching for a second. "It's simply not dripping with fat and grease from frying."

"You call medium rare *cooked*?"

"I'm going to call it cold if you don't try it soon."

Kassidy ignored the warning. Cold didn't scare her, not when there was a microwave on the counter behind her. "I guess I just prefer my burger flatter. And with more stuff on it."

"But you took off the cucumber and lettuce—"

"Not that stuff," she interrupted. "I mean lots of mustard and pink sauce."

"What's pink sauce?" Matt asked, half-convinced he didn't want to know.

"I'm not sure what they call it in the stores, but I think it's a mixture of ketchup, mayo, relish and little bits of dried onion. It really spices up a burger."

"All that stuff has fat and salt in it," Matt protested. "I just added a couple of herbs to make the flavor of the meat come out. And there's a slice of real onion there under the tomato, if you're looking for something familiar." Trying not to show his exasperation, he took a deep breath before asking, "Don't you ever eat hamburgers anywhere besides those places with plastic seats and talking French fries?"

"Of course I do," she huffed. "And if you order them right, they're okay... like well-done, with double cheese, bacon and maybe some guacamole sauce."

"I give up," he said, shaking his head in defeat. "This is supposed to be a kind of compromise," he reminded her, "and I don't think you're trying."

"I'm trying."

"No, Kassidy, you're not." And then, because he wanted her to know she wasn't the only one trying something uncharacteristic, he told her about the treat he had hidden in the refrigerator. "I've brought home double-chocolate, marshmallow-crunch ice cream," he said, tempting her with her favorite dessert.

"*You?*" she exclaimed, laughing at the look of chagrin on his face.

"I thought I might as well try it," he said wryly, "considering that's practically all you used to eat at night."

"You're a sweetie," she said with a grin, then gave the hamburger before her serious consideration. Hefting the mighty sandwich with both hands, she brought it to her lips and nibbled.

A little meat, a little bread, a little more meat. It wasn't bad, she thought, deftly avoiding the tomato as she took a more aggressive bite out of the sandwich. Certainly not up to take-out standards, but it was food . . . and it wasn't yogurt. Eyeing the pathetic inroads she'd made, Kassidy returned the hamburger to her plate and calmly smashed her palm on top.

The entire thing squashed down at least two inches, with the tomato shooting out the side as a bonus. Satisfied now that it was beginning to look like something familiar, Kassidy opened her mouth wide and took an enormous bite.

It was, well, okay. In fact, it was better than okay, now that she'd tamed it. Chewing more enthusiastically, she smiled at Matt and reminded herself to tell him it wasn't nearly as bad as she'd expected.

"You can always eat the tomato later," Matt proposed, carefully not flinching as she desecrated his culinary masterpiece. As long as she ate it, he supposed it didn't matter what it looked like!

"Just because I'm eating this doesn't mean I'll eat tofu," Kassidy said between bites.

Matt just laughed. "I wouldn't dream of asking that of you."

"COMPROMISE ISN'T SO HARD," Kassidy said later, when they were turning out the lights before retiring upstairs. "We've gone a whole day now, and just look at what we've accomplished—I got home from work before you, we ate a meal together, and we didn't fight once!"

"Probably because we're both trying," Matt said across the darkened kitchen as he waited for her in the moonlight.

But would there come a time when they *quit* trying? Kassidy had to wonder as she crossed to take Matt's hand for the walk upstairs.

8

IT WAS FOUR FORTY-FIVE before Kassidy rounded the corner of the bank in the final sprint for home. Pushing the gas pedal closer to the floor, she tried to convince herself Matt wouldn't mind, that it was the first time she'd been late all week.

But he would mind, because that was a lie. Today, Friday, was the third day she'd arrived home after four, and the only excuse she had was that she'd been putting together a proposal for a new client and the time had gotten away from her. At least she hadn't brought the proposal home with her, she'd tell him. And that was the truth, strictly speaking. To be sure, her briefcase was filled with all sorts of work, but none of it had anything to do with the new client. She had high hopes of getting most of it done while Matt was off playing golf or whatever that weekend. Besides, she defended herself, nothing had been said about not bringing work home.

Still, she wasn't about to tell him if he didn't ask.

Kassidy sighed, rubbing her fingers across her brow as she tried to figure out how she could possibly have thought that changing her approach to work would be easy.

Monday hadn't been too bad, mostly because it had been her first day to leave at an early hour and the work she hadn't accomplished didn't show up until Tuesday.

And while the second day hadn't been as simple as the first, she'd still managed to make it home before three. It hadn't been too difficult to justify leaving early then, mostly because she'd still had to organize the kitchen for the cookie bake that night.

But that was still two afternoons she'd lost—opportunities for making cold calls to new clients, time in which she could have done even more research to supplement her already bulging files on various stocks. While the number of clients she handled was quite large, Kassidy never stopped trying to win more, always working at peak capacity as she serviced the needs of old customers and researched the requirements of new ones. And when the market was open she had to give it her full attention.

Wednesday had found her investigating a new biotech firm. It was working on a new process that would enable bacteria to produce a growth hormone for cattle. The time had been well spent, because she'd discovered that while the process had lots of potential applications, the management of the firm was weak. This would weigh heavily in her recommendations regarding their stock, particularly in the light of its erratic performance in the two weeks since it had been listed on the New York Stock Exchange.

Then on Thursday, SunTec—an older electronics firm she'd recommended several years ago—had jumped eight points, and she'd had to call half a dozen clients to see if they wanted to sell when the market opened the next morning. She didn't recommend selling, but the calls needed to be made, because anytime a stock jumped twenty percent in one day, sell orders had to be reevaluated. There were other clients she hadn't called, because the nature of their contract was based upon leaving all the decisions up to her. She preferred things that way, although the tension of having that much responsibility vied with the thrill of making winning decisions.

Kassidy pulled into the driveway, pumping the brakes furiously when the car appeared not to notice her first command to stop. About three inches from the garage door, it screeched to a shuddering stop. She breathed a sigh of relief, then grabbed a pad from the console and made a note to call the garage about getting the brakes fixed. Too bad they hadn't acted up yesterday, she mused, knowing she hadn't a prayer of getting her mechanic to look at them until the weekend was over. Pushing the note into the paper clip that was on her visor, Kassidy crawled out of the car and hotfooted it into the house.

Total silence greeted her when she closed the front door behind her. Spurred on by the sudden hope that she'd gotten lucky, Kassidy looked for other clues, like a stack of dishes in the kitchen sink. There were none. None on the counter, either. She retreated to the library where she tossed her briefcase onto the sofa and ran up the stairs to their room.

The bed was made. And there were no clothes on the floor, nor were there any wet towels draped over the bathtub.

Somehow she'd managed to beat him home! Now only *she* knew she'd been late, that she'd not kept up her side of the bargain about working through the late-afternoon hours. Trying to convince herself that it was a victory, she pulled off the light wool skirt and silk blouse, grabbing a pair of shorts and T-shirt from the middle drawer. It *was* a victory, she insisted as she folded the blouse to lay it on the pile for dry cleaning. She'd managed to get home before Matt, so if she hadn't quite lived up to her promise, no one was hurt.

So why didn't it feel good?

Irritated that she couldn't shrug off the unease, Kassidy moved into the bathroom and reached for her hairbrush. Dragging the soft bristles through her hair, she studied her reflection.

"You know what it is, don't you?" she told her reflection. And she did, too, because what she saw in the mirror was plain as day. Guilt, with a capital G.

"So what are you going to do about it?" she demanded. "Are you going to tell him, so he knows how weak you are . . . that you can't keep your promises?"

She didn't want to do that, not today when he'd made such efforts to leave the house neat and tidy. And today wasn't the first day he'd done it. Yesterday she'd been just as surprised, just as shocked that the house was clean when she arrived home—so clean that she hadn't bothered with any of the chores she'd planned for the evening, like cleaning the bathroom. It was already spotless when she walked in with rubber gloves and three kinds of cleansers.

Somehow she couldn't imagine Matt scrubbing toilets, but he must have done, because the bathroom was clean and she hadn't done it.

It made being late home from work all the worse. Kassidy threw her brush into the top drawer and stalked out of the bathroom. She'd do better next week, she promised herself as she looked out the window at the pool she hadn't been near since Monday. She'd do better, she repeated.

She had to.

THE WEEKEND got off to a racing start when Matt practically flew into the house and found her waiting. There was a game, he said, dragging her out the front door. Softball, he told her when she asked, although she would have gone anywhere he asked, just to be with him.

So they went to the softball game—he played, she didn't—and then on to a movie after a quick dinner at her favorite seafood place. Saturday was just as frantic, with her story hour, his Little League, their barbecue in the backyard for a dozen or so friends. It had been exciting being with Matt, at home with him and surrounded by people who had known them when they were a married couple...people who had introduced them at a similar party not so very long ago.

Sunday was slower, much slower, especially in the morning when Matt finally got out of bed and returned with a breakfast tray that they shared among the sheets and pillows. And then, while Matt was getting ready to leave for his golf game, Kassidy changed the sheets, because the only thing she hated more than wrinkled sheets were crumby ones!

She didn't want him to play golf, because it was so very comforting to have him near, but the minute he walked out the front door, Kassidy headed for the library and her briefcase and, for a while, forgot all about the wonderful hopes and dreams and secrets he'd whispered into her ear in the darkness of night.

It was a wonderful weekend.

THE TELEPHONE RANG as Kassidy was debating the merits of putting through a sell order or holding on to it for another hour. Normally, when a client told her to sell, she sold. Pronto.

But she had a feeling about this one....

Matt's voice on the other end of the line renewed her feeling that she ought to wait. Otherwise, why had the call come in at a decision point? She grinned, knowing most people in the business would laugh at her superstitious approach. But it was just a part of what went into her knack for buying and selling at the most advantageous times. And it was the reason she got paid the big bucks. She was right more often than she was wrong.

Kassidy went with her gut feeling, putting the order in front of her computer so as not to forget about it. Another hour, she decided, and then she'd sell. In the meantime, she keyed the stock's call letters into her computer so she could keep an eye on the most current quote, just in case.

Eyes on the flashing screen, she dragged her attention back to Matt. "What did you say?"

"You mean, besides hello, how are you, let's have lunch?"

His voice sent sparks of excitement clear down to her toes, and she kicked off her shoes under her desk to rub the soles of her feet on the carpet. Just hearing his voice did this to her, she realized. It turned her into a mass of nerve endings and electrical impulses. She wasn't supposed to be feeling this way, she thought, not after the long weekend they'd spent together. She needed rest, not more of the erotic stimulation Matt was so good at.

Obviously her body disagreed.

"Now?" Kassidy checked the bank of clocks, having trouble locating the one she needed. Matt did that to her, made her disoriented and clumsy and a little out of focus. It wasn't a bad feeling, but certainly didn't have a place at work. She shook her head until it rattled, then concentrated on the clock that displayed Pacific Daylight Time. "Ten-thirty?"

"I was thinking closer to eleven."

That shivery feeling again. Kassidy shoved her feet back into her shoes, knowing the quivering wouldn't stop until he was off the phone, wondering if Matt had the slightest idea of how she trembled just hearing his voice.

At least he wasn't here beside her desk, she consoled herself. Her reaction to Matt in person was much worse. Clearing her throat in an attempt to regain her equilibrium, she tried to remember that he was only on the phone. "This stockbroker doesn't have lunch until the market is closed," she said. "And I'm meeting a client then, so you're out of luck."

"No wonder you're always bringing home those little white bags full of stuff you didn't eat. You're so busy working, you forget you're in a restaurant."

"I like leftovers," she returned. "They make great snacks."

Matt thought about the increasing number of doggie bags inhabiting the refrigerator, and wondered if they needed to get a dog to go with them. "So, no lunch. I guess you'll have to wait until you come home for your surprise."

Come home. Kassidy felt her throat constrict; he said the words so easily. *Come home.* Seeking a distraction, Kassidy tapped one of the computer keys and watched as the quote was updated. Nothing yet.

Again she felt good about herself, especially after two days of successfully arriving home by three-thirty. True, she'd promised to try for two or three o'clock, but was still very proud of herself for doing as well as she had. It had been especially rewarding because Matt had been there, waiting for her, and they'd spent every minute together.

"You're just trying to make sure I don't work late," she accused, smiling as she wondered what kind of surprise he'd arranged.

"Nonsense," he returned. "I'm genuinely disappointed you can't have lunch with me so I could tell you then."

"So tell me now." Her finger nervously tapped the key again, revealing a tiny, upward change to the quote. An insignificant change, she thought. But she kept her finger on the key, knowing that if it changed again, her instinct would be proved right.

"It's not as good that way," he drawled, sending a new wave of shivers through her body. "I like to watch your face when you're . . . surprised."

He'd said the same thing last night, she remembered. Well, nearly the same thing. "I like to watch your face . . . when I'm inside you . . . when you're out of control." Kassidy was just about ready to agree to anything, everything, when her finger reflexively hit the key again. The stock had moved.

It was a small step, she admitted, but enough to earn her attention. "You'll just have to suffer," she said, both hands on the keyboard now, the telephone hooked on her shoulder. "Think how much better it will be if you have to wait for it," she teased, grinning when his groan came across the line, loud and clear. Satisfied that she was leaving him both aroused and frustrated, Kassidy said a firm goodbye and focused all her attention on the screen in front of her.

"A JACUZZI?"

"Hot tub, actually." Grinning at her from the gazebolike enclosure beside the lawn, Matt rocked back and forth on his feet as he enjoyed the surprise and bewilderment on her face. "Like it?"

"I don't know," she said, eyes wide as she mounted the steps to look inside. "How much did it cost?"

"Now how did I know that would be your first question?" Matt shook his head in mock disappointment, watching with genuine amusement as Kassidy stepped cautiously onto the wood decking that encircled the Plexiglas tub. He could see why she was so surprised. It had taken an enormous effort to coordinate the construction, particularly since he'd wanted to keep it a surprise.

Last night had been the tricky part, with the half-finished frame in full view of the house and construction materials littering the yard. But he'd planned well, lying in wait for her when she returned from work, rushing her out of the house before she could do much more than drop her briefcase, taking her shopping, because he insisted she needed something sleek and glamorous and new for an upcoming awards banquet he wanted her to attend, and keeping her out for dinner against all her protests that it was too expensive, the middle of the week, etc. And then, when it was night, he'd brought her home and made love to her in the dark because light streaming from the back windows would have spotlighted what he was trying to hide.

This morning had been worse. He'd rolled out of bed the second her alarm sounded, pretending an awakeness he didn't feel, diverting her attention from the windows as she dressed, following her down the stairs, nearly frantic as she poured juice and tried to sit in the breakfast nook to read the newspaper—the nook with all the windows that, naturally, faced the backyard.

She'd stepped on his bare toes at least once as he'd blocked her line of vision. He'd responded with cuddling and kisses, anything to keep her from questioning his odd behavior. And when he'd finally shut the front door behind her, he'd kept watch through a window to make sure she didn't double back and ruin everything.

Against all odds, she was surprised. "Of course it's my first question," she said, her gaze drawn to the roomy tub with its submerged, benchlike seat. "Hot tubs are expensive."

"On the contrary. Building this was a cost-effective decision," Matt told her, crossing the few steps to where Kassidy still stood, a little stunned, he thought. Running a comforting hand up and down her back, he wondered how long she'd talk about it before ripping off her clothes and diving in. He could tell she liked it, knew by the way she was studying every inch of the enclosure that his impulse had been a good one. All he had to do now was let her rationalize it. "It was either this or sell the family silver in order to offset the cost of heating the pool. The hot tub made more sense."

"We don't have any family silver," she reminded him, leaning back into his embrace. "And I'd already decided not to mess with the thermostat anymore. I told you that."

"Does this mean you don't want it?" he murmured into her ear, his tongue drawing a wet path along the outer curve. He felt the shiver that shot through her, knew she'd felt his own.

"I guess it can stay," she said, knowing her badly feigned reluctance was a clear giveaway of her delight. "At least I don't have to worry anymore about having you committed."

"Committed?"

"Admit it," she demanded, turning in his arms until the tips of her breasts were drilling his chest and her flat tummy could further heat the swelling hardness behind the harsh barrier of his jeans. He gasped, she smiled. "You were acting pretty crazy this morning."

"And last night?" Matt wondered how soon she'd guessed he'd had something to hide, smiling a little when he realized how silly he must have looked once she'd realized he was up to something. Then he moaned as she threaded her fingers into his hair and pulled.

It was a sensual hurt, one that was designed to arouse and excite, made more exciting when she drew his bottom lip between her teeth and bit softly. He wanted her then, here, now...it didn't matter. Neighbors be damned, his body was *demanding* to invade hers.

She laughed softly against his still-tingling lips, reminding him of last night, when those lips had stroked and smiled and teased their way across every inch of his body. She'd laughed in her pleasure, knowing the beads of sweat that covered him were there because she'd made it so.

"How did I know?" she repeated, nibbling again, because she loved the taste of his mouth. "Besides the part where you let *me* pick the restaurant?" She laughed again, loving his chagrined expression and not wanting a thing to ever change him. "Or was it when you didn't say a single word about how many weeks' worth of cholesterol rations you were consuming in one night?" she asked, swaying closer to his heat as his hands came to rest on the curves of her fanny. She gasped a little when his fingers dug into the soft flesh there, found herself wishing for more privacy than the open portal of the hot tub. Maybe in the tub itself . . .

"I guess I wasn't real smooth," he admitted, grateful he was now wearing shoes when her toes stepped onto his once again, and then ran out of breath as she used the added height to rub her pelvis against his hard arousal.

"Oh, you were smooth, lover." She breathed the words into his mouth, her tongue darting inside for the full flavor of him. "Even when you were rough, you were smooth. Hot and hard . . . and so very, very smooth." She took a deep breath, gasped when his teeth closed on the tender skin at her neck, then cried out when his hot tongue laved the non-existent wound.

"Let's go—"

"I can't!" she cried, wishing her legs could support her, knowing they wouldn't.

"We can't do it here!" he ground out, steeling himself to step back, hurting with every inch he put between them. It would just take a few steps, he told himself, and then they'd be in the kitchen. Sixty feet, he figured. Twenty seconds, max.

Whisking Kassidy into his arms, Matt tried for ten.

"How do you like the hot tub?"

"I like it," she said, the words a tremulous sigh as she leaned against the cushioned backrest. Letting her body rise and float at the whim of the steady blast of water from the submerged jets, Kassidy wondered how much better life could get. "I like it a lot."

"I guess we can keep it, then," Matt said, reaching down from the lounger he'd pulled into the gazebo to pop another grape into her mouth. "For a minute there, though, you had me worried."

"I'll bet," she snorted before closing her lips over the sweet grape. "You were just afraid I'd make you tell me what it cost."

"You'll find out," he said and chuckled, wondering how well Kassidy would take the joke when she discovered the bill was addressed to her. He laughed harder, feeling anticipation mix with a pleasurable dread as he looked forward to the scene.

He knew it would be interesting. He was pretty confident about the outcome, though. Kassidy seemed to really like the sizzling spa.

"You're either laughing because you've got another scheme up your sleeve, or I'm turning lobster red and you think it's amusing." Lifting heavy eyelids, Kassidy challenged the man lying high and dry near her head. "Which is it, buster?"

"Both, I'm afraid," he told her, loving her more now than he had just moments ago, no longer wondering why things kept getting better. They hadn't argued about the hot tub, about dinner the night before . . . not even about the book Kassidy had destroyed the other night when she'd browsed through it.

"I can't believe you're not even going to put your toe in the water," she said, relaxing again without waiting for his answer. If he had another surprise, she thought she could handle it, especially if it was as nice as this one. As long as it wasn't too expensive, she added silently.

"Those things sap your energy," he said, eyeing the roiling waters with distaste. "Besides, it's more fun watching you from up here."

"The view's better?" she asked, feeling decadently risqué as she floated practically naked in the tub, her minuscule bikini better suited to the coast of France than the Pacific Northwest.

"The view's better," he confirmed, leering wickedly at her from his sybaritic pose, laughing when she blushed. "And this way I can look all I want without taking a chance you'll seduce me."

"I can seduce you without breathing," she said huskily, rolling over to rest her elbows on the edge, propping her chin upon her hands. "But I've got a couple of other things I want to talk about, so you're off the hook . . . for now."

"What other things?" he asked, mesmerized by the promise of passion in her sparkling eyes.

"The house, for one," she said. "I think you're doing too much of the cleaning." Stopping his protest with a simple hand signal, she continued. "Every time I've come home lately, it's all clean. Not just picked up, but sparkling clean! You've gone from a slob to Mr. Clean in a week."

"You don't like it?" he asked, uneasily aware the jig was up. Lenore, the maid, had been working a week now, and he'd been trying to figure out how to break the news to Kassidy.

"I like it," she said with a grin, "but I'm not doing anything to help and that's not fair. What I want to tell you is to leave some things for me, and I'll take care of them on the weekends."

He was tempted to tell Lenore just that, to leave a few little things for Kassidy to clean, but he knew he was going to get caught someday and figured it was better to come clean now. Grimacing at the pun, Matt sighed heavily and looked over her head so he didn't have to see the disappointment in her eyes. "I got us a maid."

"You've got a *what?*" she asked, not sure she was hearing correctly.

"A maid. Hired her last week. She works about three hours most weekdays." He still didn't look at her, preferring instead to admire the intricate latticework of the gazebo. "It's not like we can't afford it!"

A maid. Kassidy felt the anger build and did nothing to stop it. He hadn't compromised, not at all. He was still a slob, and he was spending more money to stay that way.

It was unacceptable.

On the other hand, it could also work to her advantage. A brilliant idea struck her without warning, and she had to work hard not to smile at the equity of it. Behind closed lids, Kassidy worked furiously on her calculations, adding the pluses and minuses until she thought there was some kind of a balance. A precarious one, she admitted, but a balance, nevertheless.

"If you've hired a maid, I assume that means I no longer have to keep up my side of the cleaning," she began, eyeing him coldly for any hint of suspicion. There wasn't any. He just nodded.

"So I could probably sneak in an extra hour or so of work here and there," she said smoothly, smiling a little when he flinched. He deserved it, she thought, for going behind her back.

"Once in a while," he said, because there was no other way out of the corner he'd painted himself into. "But not every day," he insisted, relieved when she nodded ever so slightly.

Kassidy struck with part two of her bargain. "And if there's now a maid in the budget, we have to find a way to pay her."

"We don't have a budget," he said, still awfully surprised she wasn't ranting and raving or just plain arguing. Until she raised her voice, Matt figured he was in the clear.

"Not yet," she said. "But we need one." Standing on the submerged shelf of the pool, she reached for a towel and began drying herself. "We need a budget that includes expenses and monthly commitments toward investments."

"Because of a maid?" Matt asked, suddenly realizing he was getting suckered into more than he'd expected.

"If you want a maid, I want a budget," she said smoothly, stepping from the pool to sit on a nearby garden chair. Drying her calves with slow, stroking motions, she explained. "You know it's important to me to have a plan for the future. I've always had a budget, a financial plan. Now we're both going to have one."

Figuring he could kiss off that new car he'd seen on the lot the other day, Matt agreed with a nod. He'd known since she moved in that the money problem was going to come up, but it didn't look too bad. At least, not yet. "So we're not going to argue?" he asked, standing up and crossing to her chair.

"Not if you're reasonable about this," she said. "I'll have my financial consultant come over one night soon, and we'll have a look at what we can do."

She looked like the cat that swallowed the canary, smug and triumphant. Matt knew then that he'd been outmaneuvered, but it didn't seem to matter. Kassidy was happy, winning something he'd always intended to give her.

Together they grabbed the cover for the hot tub, lowered it until one side was covered, working together to flip the other half across. It was an anticlimax, Matt told himself, a letdown, because Kassidy hadn't fought, they hadn't fought. And he must have expected the fight, some sort of an argument, because it didn't feel complete. The maid, the hot tub, a budget ... So many new things between them, changes that seemed to imply other changes, links that bound them to a future neither could foresee.

"There's one thing, Kassidy," he said, hesitating just a little because he didn't want to bring it up, but knowing it had to be done.

"What's that?" she asked, her head full of schemes that would provide a wonderful future for the two of them.

"What if it doesn't work?" he asked, stepping down to the grass, where she waited for him. Bringing her close against his side with an arm around her shoulders, he asked again, "What do we do if it doesn't work?"

"The budget?" Flashing a questioning glance at him, she was startled to find he wasn't smiling. Instead, he was showing a concern that was much too grave for the subject, especially after his ready acceptance of her proposal.

"Not the budget," he said softly. "Us."

HE COULDN'T have been serious, she decided.

But for a moment there her heart had stopped. They had too much going for them this time. They were learning, trying not to fight, even though sometimes it was a lot like walking on eggs. Like the other day when she'd tried to skim a couple of pages of Matt's new book, and the back had cracked the moment she touched it. He hadn't yelled at her, not then, not even later when she'd spilled a little iced tea onto the cover.

He'd wanted to yell and she knew it. But even if he had yelled, it was too late for that book, and there was nothing either of them could do about it. Still, she wished she'd been just a little more careful, because Matt had been so wonderful about not noticing when she took a couple of free minutes to read through some files from her briefcase the other night.

No, he couldn't possibly have doubts about whether they'd make it together. She wouldn't let him.

Hearing his footsteps coming down the hall, she practiced the best smile she had and flashed it at him as he came into the kitchen. "I've got Girl Scouts at seven," Kassidy reminded him as she rummaged inside the refrigerator for something to eat. "We're baking cookies tonight."

"And that's an excuse not to have dinner?" he asked as though uncertain he'd heard her properly. "More cookies?"

"That's right," she agreed, peeking inside first one then another doggie bag until she found what she was looking for. "And I can't eat a real meal because I won't have time. I was supposed to find Mom's chocolate chip recipe last night, but I forgot. Now I'll have to call her, and you know how long that takes!" Pulling a long, burrito-shaped thing from the sack, Kassidy held it delicately between two fingers as she tore off a square of paper towel with the other hand. Then she set the whole thing in the microwave and punched out a couple of numbers. "On top of everything else, Millie's on vacation, so I'll be on my own."

"Don't you think a plate would work better?" Matt inquired, squinting into the shadowed interior as the limp, greasy thing sputtered and spat on the revolving platter.

"This is faster," she said, tossing the paper sack back into the refrigerator and plucking out a diet soft drink before kicking the door shut.

"That stuff will make your stomach curdle," Matt promised blackly as he shrugged into his lightweight jacket. Giving her a quick peck on the cheek, he headed for the back door.

"Only if I eat it slow," she told him with a grin. "The object lesson is to overwhelm my stomach before it knows what's happening. Then it's too late to argue."

"I seriously doubt if you've ever considered your stomach at all," Matt said, opening the door as Kassidy opened the microwave. "I'll leave you girls to your cooking and see if I can find something to eat at Charlie's. We're meeting with the other team coaches and managers tonight. See you later."

"See you later," she echoed, biting into the soft, lukewarm burrito as he hurried to the garage. Delighted with her victory—there was always a chance Matt would insist on a proper meal—she wrapped another square of paper towel around the dripping burrito and picked up the phone to call her mother.

It wasn't the first time she'd called her since her address had changed, but Amanda Canyon's enthusiasm hadn't waned in the least. With a mouth full of burrito, Kassidy responded to the same questions her mother had asked every time, giving mostly the same answers. Yes, she was working less. No, Matt hadn't minded when she brought a little work home. Yes, he was being less of a slob, and oh, by the way, he'd hired a maid.

"He seems to be enjoying it more," Kassidy said about Matt's work, "and he's a lot more consistent about going into the store. I guess he's gotten out of the funk he was in about working."

"Are you sure you're working less?" she asked.

"What's the matter, Mom?" Kassidy asked, impatient with both the subject and her parent. "Can't you take my word for it?"

"Don't snap at me, Kassidy," her mother said, not at all put off by her daughter's irritation. "I'm the one who tried to get you to take summers off during college, remember? But you insisted on taking summer classes and working. And you wouldn't listen to me, because it interfered with whatever grand scheme you had in mind. Somehow I can't believe you'll let things change that easily, not even for Matt."

Kassidy didn't reply, not right away. Amanda was right, and it was hard to admit it to her, much less to herself. She hadn't changed, not that much, certainly not as much as she'd promised Matt. But she would try harder, she promised herself.

"Maybe I'll have better luck next week," was all she said to her mom.

"What about that promotion you told me about last week?"

Amanda Canyon certainly had a way of sticking to a subject! Kassidy took a short, deep breath before answering. "I'm not sure it's one I want. For one thing, it'll mean more management responsibilities. And I can't figure how I'll fit that in and still keep the same clients and cut down on the hours I put in at the office."

"So you're thinking of turning it down?"

"I'm still thinking it over," Kassidy said, refusing to be cornered into answering. And then, because she wanted to change the subject, she said, "Remember that wonderful chocolate chip recipe that you used to make when I was a little girl?"

"Of course I remember," her mom said, her tone of voice indicating she was not hoodwinked into believing Kassidy was being charming for the sake of it. "I give you that recipe every year."

"And every year I lose it," Kassidy agreed, knowing that if she looked hard enough, she'd discover a number of the missing copies among her papers in the library. But she didn't have time to sort through them tonight, not with the Scouts due so soon. "It's just because we're still a little confused over here after the move," she said, trying for an excuse, playing on her mother's delight at their decision to try living together. "There are still a lot of things I need to sort through."

"And you imagine you have all the time in the world to take care of that," Amanda observed. "Your confidence about your and Matt's future would be pretty overwhelming if I didn't know how hard you were trying."

The sarcasm almost sent her over the edge. "I thought we dropped that subject, Mom."

"You dropped it, dear. I'm just being a nosy mother." And before Kassidy could decide whether she was going to fight or agree, Amanda returned to the subject of the cookies. "I'm really surprised my efficient daughter can't manage to keep a recipe from one year to the next."

Kassidy was so grateful she didn't have to talk about Matt again that she ignored her mother's unveiled criticism. "I keep trying to remember to put it into my cookbook—"

"What cookbook?" Amanda interrupted.

"That was low, Mom," she said darkly, then began scribbling as the recipe was dictated. Hanging up on her mother after a hasty word of thanks that was designed to forestall any further conversation, Kassidy checked the cupboards and made another list for the store. She had half an hour, she figured as she ran out the front door and down the walk to her car.

Timesaving habits, such as leaving the keys in her car, really came in handy at moments like these, Kassidy thought as she flung her purse into the back seat and pulled shut the door. Priming the carburetor by pumping the gas pedal a couple of times, Kassidy then turned the key.

And got nothing. No humming of working parts, no gentle coughing of a reluctant engine. Not even a wheeze or two. Her car, for better or worse, was dead.

She tried the process again, this time beating on the dashboard, as though the disciplinary measure would influence anything. Again, nothing. "That figures!" she muttered aloud. "First the brakes, now this!"

Kassidy jumped out of the car, grabbed her purse and kicked a tire before retreating up the concrete walk. She needed eggs, flour, chocolate chips and pecans, enough for twenty dozen cookies, and the store was half a mile away. Much too far to walk, she grumbled, dreading the effort even as she approached the front door. She needed to change her shoes first, she told herself. Sandals would slow her down.

A flash of blue caught her eye as she pushed the key into the front-door lock. She turned her head a little, toward the driveway, where the sun was glistening on the roof of Matt's new sports car.

He must have taken his bike, she thought, her mind leaping ahead as she tried to remember where Matt kept his spare keys. Dashing into the library, she pulled open the desk drawer and found an assortment of keys. Kassidy grabbed the one with the Mercedes-Benz key chain that was obviously meant for the hot little car in the driveway and ran back outside.

Bless Matt for being an exercise nut and leaving his car at home! she thought gleefully as she revved the powerful motor and played with the gearshift. Satisfied she could control it at least long enough to drive to the store and back, she squealed out of the driveway.

Responsive! she noticed as the car tore down the street at only the slightest pressure on the pedal. And she wasn't quite used to the way it turned, although she soon got the knack of it after cutting in too quickly and ending up grazing the curb a time or two.

Her experience as a passenger in this car hadn't been nearly as exciting as driving it, and she kind of thought she could get used to driving a car that smelled as good as it looked. Personally, though, she thought she'd prefer something in a fire-engine red. A convertible, perhaps, she mused as she bounced the little car over a dip and into the parking lot.

It was a thought.

9

"REMEMBER, GIRLS, we're doing this again tomorrow. We promised the Rotary Club we'd bake enough for their picnic."

"How long do you think it'll take?" one of the Scouts asked as they sorted through the sweaters and jackets piled on the hallway chair.

"Two or three hours," Kassidy said, crossing her fingers. "But that's only if everyone shows up on time and we don't burn any."

"But Kassidy!" Shelly moaned as she balanced the boxes of cookies in one arm and tried to pull on her sweater. "Karen's having her birthday party in the afternoon, and we all decided to make her one of those neat candles like you showed us last month. When are we going to have time if we're baking cookies all day?"

Kassidy grabbed the cookies before they fell, shaking her head at the chorus of agreement from the other girls. "We can do the candle here, too, but you have to promise to work fast." She returned Shelly's cookies and reached behind Carol's back to pluck her ponytail from beneath her jacket. "Be here the second I get home from story hour, and be ready!"

"Gee, thanks, Kassidy!" Shelly exclaimed, reaching up to hug her before giving way so the other girls could say their goodbyes.

"And on Saturday we'll have to arrange them on the platters so they look as good as they taste *and* deliver them to the park," Kassidy reminded them. The nine girls groaned good-naturedly and filed out the door to the waiting car pools. All of them carried plastic or tin boxes of the cookies to store temporarily in their freezers at home. Kassidy shut the door when the last one had climbed into a car, exhausted but pleased. The girls had worked hard, and they only had another fifteen or twenty dozen cookies to bake on Saturday.

Fifteen or twenty dozen! As tired as she felt tonight, the prospect boggled her mind and she collapsed against the front door, munching on a leftover cookie for energy. She was still there five minutes later when she heard the kitchen door open and shut, and listened to Matt's progress through the house. She heard him stop by the cookie jar, and was waiting for him when he strolled through the hall to where she was leaning against the door.

"That stuff will rot your arteries," she pointed out, rising onto her toes to plant a crumbly kiss upon his cheek.

"My arteries are healthy enough to stand up to a few cookies," he said, slipping his arm around her waist to pull her close. "Yours, on the other hand, are probably still shell-shocked by all the cheese and grease in that burrito. Cookies are health food compared to that."

"I suppose you have a burrito recipe that's edible?" she asked, nibbling on the cookie he held between his fingers.

"I'll make it, if you'll eat it," he challenged, snatching his fingers out of range of her mouth. "And if you want another cookie, go get your own."

Kassidy thought about it, but decided she'd probably sleep better if she didn't. But then again it was only nine-thirty and she never got to bed before eleven. Her decision made, she headed back into the kitchen.

One more cookie wouldn't hurt.

SATURDAY NIGHT was a change of pace from the daylight hours. By the time Kassidy had read three stories at the library, baked cookies and made candles with the Girl Scouts, and cheered from the stands during two Little League games, she was totally wiped out. Retreating to the library after a quick dinner—she'd made Chinese chicken salad from a recipe Marla had given her, and it was really okay as long as she didn't have to think about how good it was for you—Kassidy checked out the titles on the shelf where Matt kept spy and adventure stories. Plucking a fat, heavy volume from the shelf, she carried it to the leather sofa in front of the fireplace and settled in for a good read.

Without a second thought, she cracked open the book and flattened it on her knee.

She was deep into the second chapter when she heard Matt calling her from the other end of the house. "I'm in here!" she shouted back, returning her attention to the story. It was fascinating and a little ridiculous. Kassidy almost found herself laughing at the Cold War antics of spies and masters as they dueled from opposite sides of the Berlin Wall. Normally, the fictitious spy novel would have had her gripping the book with frenzied anxiety. Unfortunately, the author had made a very bad miscalculation.

While the book was written in the early eighties, he'd time-leaped the drama to the year 1989, the same year the infamous barrier had been torn down amid a whirlpool of delirious celebrations. Unfortunately the author hadn't had the benefit of foresight, and while he was sneaking agents back and forth through the checkpoints, real people were strolling across the borders on shopping trips and sightseeing excursions.

"Don't forget to leave me your keys so I can give them to the mechanic," Matt said from the doorway.

"They're in the car," Kassidy said without lifting her head.

"That's a good way to get your car stolen," he chided.

"Steal my car? Who are you kidding?"

He smirked, but his attention was caught by the poor, broken book on her lap. "What are you reading?"

Kassidy lifted the book, showing him the cover as she leaned over the arm of the sofa to reach for the soft drink she'd left on the table. Taking a gulp, she put it back, careful to set it on another book. She was very careful about water rings on furniture.

Matt groaned aloud as he saw the broken back of the book, then groaned again as he noticed the second book under her soft drink. It was already warped by the dewy moisture sliding from the glass, and would soon look as though it had been dropped into the bathtub.

"I thought we agreed you wouldn't break the backs on my books," he began, "and I'm not much happier having you use that one as a coaster."

Kassidy looked up in surprise, shifting her eyes from Matt to the book in her hand to the book on the table, then back to Matt. She hadn't done it consciously, but there was no way to get out of this one. "This looks to be a hard habit to break."

"*Break* is precisely the thing we're trying to avoid," he said.

"I'm not perfect, Matt," she said and sighed, becoming disheartened.

"I'm not looking for perfect, honey. I'm looking for compatible."

"I am really sorry, Matt," she said, gently pressing the book together and massaging the broken spine. "It's kind of a bad habit." Anxious to make amends, she studied the ridged back, delighted to find only one break along the surface. "See? Only one break," she showed him, smiling her delight.

He didn't say anything, so Kassidy tried again. "It could have been worse," she offered, not at all happy with the scowl on his face. "I might have made it another couple of chapters before you noticed. Then it might have really made a difference."

"You think just a little broken is going to make it better?" he asked softly, knowing he was pushing her into a corner, but not giving an inch.

Kassidy pretended to think about that one as she reached for the dripping glass. Conscientious to the last, she wiped the wet cover of the second book on her shirt and polished it with her sleeve. Satisfied that she'd repaired the damage, she tossed it back onto the table. "I guess I'll have to buy some coasters for in here. These books soak up the water like sponges. Don't do the job at all."

"Their job is to be read," Matt said evenly. "Not to be used for anything else."

"I'll bet you never pressed leaves between pages when you were a little kid," Kassidy huffed, getting just a bit hostile under his unrelenting glare.

"What has that got to do with anything?" he asked, suddenly disoriented.

Kassidy ignored his question, pressing on with the meat of her argument. "Besides, how can a person be expected to read a book when you can't even open it wide enough to see all the words?" Knowing full well she was on the wrong side, fighting a losing battle, Kassidy warmed up for the confrontation. This was an old habit, taking sides against the middle . . . especially when the middle was a muddy line.

Matt clenched his fists around the wainscoting that lined the doorway, wondering how he'd managed to accomplish the feat of arguing with Kassidy when all he'd wanted was to put away his car so they could go to bed and lie in each other's arms.

"I'm sorry," he said, full of the urgent need to stop this fight before it got out of control. "I know you didn't mean to do it. I shouldn't have overreacted like that."

"Does that mean you don't mind me reading your books?" she asked meekly, not really happy with herself at that moment. She hadn't intended to win this one…hadn't even intended to fight.

It was such a habit.

"I think this is a problem that's best avoided," he said slowly, unclenching his fists and letting them drift to his sides as he took in the disappointed look on her face. She knew she needed to offer something besides a fight, he thought, and he was satisfied with that knowledge.

Maybe he should let her come up with the solution. So far he'd been doing most of the problem solving.

"I think we can afford more than one copy of the books I want to read," she said, still thinking out the steps to her remedy. "I rarely buy hardbacks, anyway. If there's a book you know you want to keep, I'll just buy my own. But if you're going to toss it, you can let me have it first."

He smiled as he thought how much he loved her. It wasn't perfect, but it was an idea … *her* idea. He fine-tuned it a little, just to show he was in favor. "Why don't we divide the room, your books and stuff on one side, mine on the other? That way we know the rules. And if you really want to read one of mine, you'll remember to be careful because you've pulled it from one of my shelves."

"Do we draw a line down the middle?" she joked, not entirely thrilled with the prospect of divided territory. "And how do we cuddle if the couch is on your side?"

"We meet in the middle?" Half serious, half not, Matt decided enough was enough. "Deal?"

"Deal."

"In the meantime, I'll go move your car out of the way. Meet me upstairs in five minutes?" he asked, with just the tiniest note of hope in his voice. She looked so comfortable on that sofa, so settled. He wasn't sure if he'd need to bribe her to forget the book and come to bed.

"Three, and you're on," she challenged, tossing the book aside and scooting past him on bare feet to take the stairs leading to their room two at a time.

Matt was there in two.

SUNDAY MORNING, Kassidy decided it was her turn to make breakfast. Balancing the loaded tray, the Sunday paper wedged under her arm, she cautiously mounted the stairs. Reaching their bedroom without incident, she didn't mind at all when she lost her grip on the paper and let it fall all over the floor.

"You could have made two trips," Matt said from the bed, where he'd arranged the pillows so they could sit up together and enjoy the treat.

"It would have taken longer," Kassidy said, placing the tray on the bed before picking through the mess on the floor until she found the sections she wanted. Curling up on the bed next to Matt, she grabbed a bagel and spread cream cheese over it.

Matt did the same, much to Kassidy's astonishment, but she didn't say anything, because she figured he deserved a couple of vices—and as long as one of those vices was herself, nothing else mattered!

Matt was well into his second bagel when he put aside the sports section and spoke. "We need to talk about the vacation we're going to take."

"What vacation?"

"The one we're going to talk about," he said, draining the orange juice and reaching for the coffeepot. He warmed both cups and continued. "I figure it's time we had a few days off."

"I'm barely working now," Kassidy pointed out, intrigued with the idea, though she wasn't ready to admit it. "What makes you think I can afford to take any time off?"

"How long has it been since you've taken any vacation time?" he asked, knowing the answer but wanting her to admit it.

Kassidy gave his question serious consideration, a little surprised at the answer she came up with. "About two years, I guess."

Matt nodded. "You didn't even take any time off when we got married. Something about a transition at work—"

"Things were pretty messed up then," she said seriously. "The partners had just sold out to that Eastern company. We were all a little paranoid."

"Which explains why we didn't take a honeymoon," he finished, trying to lead her through this without provoking an argument. "But what about this last year? As far as I know, you've been working six, sometimes seven days a week without a break, for nearly two years."

"You have good spies," she grumbled.

"Your mother thinks there's something wrong with you," he said succinctly.

"You've been talking to my mother?" He had her full attention now. Kassidy hadn't realized that Matt was in contact with her mom and wondered if it was a new thing.

"We keep in touch," he admitted. He wouldn't make any points if he let Kassidy know Amanda Canyon had helped plan their reunion, had even made sure her house was full the night he'd tricked Kassidy with the cat. With her sister Tracy and family staying at her mother's, Kassidy hadn't been able to run home. "More to the point, she's worried about you."

"She's always thought there was something wrong with me," Kassidy said flatly. "Just because I'm the only one in my family with any ambition, she thinks I'm sick in the head."

"Maybe she'll feel better if you prove you're human and take some time off," he suggested.

"You want me to take a vacation to make my mother feel better?" Kassidy asked incredulously.

"It couldn't hurt."

"You're deranged."

"Does that mean you won't go?"

Kassidy thought about it for a long minute before replying. "If you're determined we go, then we'll do it... with one condition."

"Which is?"

"I get to pick the place." Rolling away from his suspicious gaze, Kassidy made a few rapid calculations. She could pull it off, she figured, if she set her mind to it. First, though, she had to convince Matt.

"Kassidy, your idea of a vacation is six countries in four days. That's not exactly what I had in mind." Matt had been considering a secluded bungalow on a private beach somewhere in the Caribbean. Now that positively reeked of vacation!

"I always thought it made sense to get the most out of the time available," she commented with a shrug, mentally reviewing her work schedule and pinpointing the days she could afford to be gone. About a week, she figured.

"And that's why we didn't go on a vacation when we were married," Matt grumbled. "Besides the fact I couldn't drag you away from the office, you wanted a marathon and I wanted a little relaxation."

"You can sit by the pool and drink piña coladas at home," Kassidy shot back. "I never could see the sense in paying exorbitant prices to do the same thing at a crowded hotel."

"It's a matter of style, love," he insisted. "Late dinners, dancing till dawn, breakfast in bed . . . That's what a holiday is all about."

"Then I guess you're not going to take to my idea." Feigning disappointment, Kassidy sighed loudly and let her shoulders droop a critical inch or two.

Matt counted to ten, then gave up. After all, at least she hadn't said she wouldn't go. And, he reminded himself, half a compromise was better than none at all. "I'll go," he said, closing his lips over a wedge of pineapple. "And I'll like it. I promise." He ate some more pineapple. Maybe with enough Vitamin C in his system, he'd be able to keep up with whatever whirlwind schedule she devised.

Keep up was the operative phrase. Enjoying it was out of the question. He hated the intense schedules that dragged tourists through the maximum number of sights in the minimum amount of time.

Kassidy decided he'd suffered enough. Flipping back over until she was looking up at him again, she made her proposal. "I kind of thought it would be fun to go hiking."

"Hiking?"

"As in camping, or whatever." Kassidy wasn't sure what it was called. She'd never done it before. To put an even finer point on the matter, she'd never even *considered* doing it!

"You want to go camping with me?" Matt was having a little trouble. He could have sworn Kassidy had just offered to go camping. "Are we talking about the same thing here? As in fresh air, open skies, cooking over a camp fire?"

"Whatever." Kassidy shrugged her shoulders once again. "You're the expert. I just thought you might like to spend a little time showing me what attracts you to the big out-of-doors."

"You never cared before," he said slowly, eyes narrowing at the flicker of pain that crossed her expression.

"I cared," she said softly. "I was just too busy to show it."

Matt was stunned. Never, not once, had Kassidy admitted to being too busy. Busy, yes, but never *too* busy.

It was a turning point.

MATT OFFERED to make homemade burritos for dinner, and Kassidy agreed to eat them.

Settling down at the table, she assessed the selection of fillings with a jaded eye. Tomato, lettuce, onion—and something that resembled refried beans. She knew better, of course. Matt would never fry anything. There were also bowls of chopped olives, shredded cheese, *salsa* and...sour cream? That would make two vices in one day for Matt. Quite a record, Kassidy mused.

"Sour cream?" she asked, dipping her finger into the white goo for a quick taste.

Matt looked over his shoulder, grinning at the look of amazement in her eyes. "That one is. I bought it for you." He pointed to another small bowl near his own plate. "The other is mock sour cream."

"Mock sour cream?" As in mock turtle soup? she wondered. Ugh!

"Low-fat cottage cheese, a little lemon, blended. It tastes pretty close and doesn't—"

"Let me guess," she interrupted, thinking about trying it just to prove he was wrong. "It tastes pretty close and doesn't have the calories of the real thing."

"Or the cholesterol. That's really more important."

Kassidy waited until his back was turned again before dipping her finger into the mock stuff. Her tongue cautiously reached out for a taste. It wasn't bad, she decided. It wasn't sour cream, but it wasn't bad. She wondered how it would taste if she used it to make her favorite French onion dip. The incongruity of the mixture of potato chips and a semi-healthy dip didn't occur to her.

Matt pretended he hadn't noticed her experiment when he crossed to the table. He put a bowl of shredded chicken onto a hot pad, then returned to the microwave for the flour tortillas. They were wrapped in a dish towel, steaming and soft.

"I've never made these at home," Kassidy admitted, centering the tortilla on her plate and piling scoops of everything on top. "Tacos, yes. But I've never made burritos."

"Obviously," he joked. "You'll never get that folded if you keep dumping stuff on it."

"I like a little of everything," she insisted, dumping a spoonful of olives in the center as a final touch.

Matt smirked, contemplating the inevitable, forthcoming disaster as he deftly rolled and folded the shell on his own plate. With a couple of practiced movements, he had a regulation burrito in one hand. Picking up a bottle of Mexican beer with the other, he accepted her halfhearted applause with a modicum of humility.

Kassidy tackled her own plate, first rolling the floppy shell right to left, then trying bottom to top. It wouldn't roll, much less fold. Determined to emerge from the fiasco with her pride intact, she snagged a tortilla chip from the basket on the table and scooped it into the filling. She ate several mouthfuls that way, reducing the mound of filling on the tortilla with every bite.

"And that's another way to do it," Matt teased, watching as Kassidy tried again to roll the burrito. She succeeded this time, but forgot to fold up the bottom part, which meant everything started to fall out as she took her first bite. He stuffed his mouth with food to keep from laughing.

"I suppose we should talk about the vacation some more," he said, finishing his first burrito and organizing a second. "I think it's sweet of you to suggest camping, but you can't be serious."

"Why not?"

"Because camping means no showers, no electricity, no fast food. That's why."

"And you think I couldn't survive without my hair dryer, I suppose," she returned a little snidely, hiding her own trepidation at the thought. A full week without a telephone? Talk about serious consequences!

"I didn't say that. It's just that you've never seemed like the kind of person who would enjoy roughing it."

"I married you, didn't I?" she challenged him with a smile. Kassidy was determined now, particularly as Matt seemed to think she'd never survive without the rudiments of civilization. She'd show him!

Matt stopped what he was doing and threw the challenge right back at her, shifting the tone of their discussion from teasing to provocative. "I thought you said I was smooth," he purred.

Seeing his eyes heat with a sensual dare, Kassidy reached for her beer and took a swig straight from the bottle. A second swig, then she fixed her eyes on the half-eaten burrito in her other hand. "I suppose it wouldn't help if I took that back?" she asked, nibbling from the burrito as she tried to avoid glancing across the table. Kassidy knew better than to look at Matt again, if she wanted to finish her dinner. Changing the subject seemed to be a reasonable tactic. "These are good. We should have them more often."

Matt took the diversion with good grace. "Glad you approve. Another beer?" he proposed, pulling out a single bottle from the refrigerator when she shook her head. "Back to the vacation, then. It sounds as though you're pretty determined to make the supreme sacrifice and revert to the wilds."

"It's not a sacrifice. It's curiosity. I figure once I've tried it, I can say definitely whether or not I like it. And if I don't, we'll work around it." Licking her fingers because she'd forgotten to put out the napkins when she set the table, Kassidy outlined her proposal. "I'm pretty sure I can get a week off, about two weeks from now. Will that be enough?"

Matt seriously doubted whether Kassidy would survive an entire week with Mother Nature. "I think three days is enough for a beginner," he said. "Maybe after that we'll do something decadent and easy." Without giving her a chance to argue about his suggestion, he pressed on. "Two weeks from now is perfect. That'll give us enough time to get you outfitted. And you'll have to break in your boots."

"Sounds like fun." Break in her boots? Kassidy kept a bland smile on her face as Matt listed everything that needed to be done in the interim, studiously ignoring the tiny pricks of panic that were attacking her psyche. A weekend in the woods. What on earth had gotten into her?

LATER THAT NIGHT, Kassidy snuggled into Matt's warmth.

"Kassidy?"

"Mmm?"

"If this doesn't work, it won't make any difference."

"To what?" She was floating, drifting between awareness and sleep, not really interested in anything more than the warm arms that held her close, the steady beat of his heart next to hers.

"To anything."

"'Kay." She didn't have a clue what he was talking about. And it didn't matter, because agreeing with him meant she didn't have to wake up.

Matt relaxed. It wouldn't work, he knew. The camping trip was a disaster in the making. Kassidy just wasn't designed to be an outdoor-type person.

But it wouldn't matter, because they'd found out their differences no longer counted. It was only *fighting* about them that had hurt. Learning to live with them was the key here.

Once Kassidy discovered she hated camping, they could both live with that. Matt was sure of it.

10

"WARREN, I can't believe you're giving up so easily!"

Kassidy quickly pushed some papers aside so Warren could perch on the side of her desk. Her eyes on the computer screen, she divided her attention between the closing minutes of the NYSE and Warren's supposedly failing love affair.

"When a woman tells you she can't go out because she can't find a sitter for her dogs, it doesn't matter whether I take her word for it or not," Warren said with just a tinge of irritation. "Millie doesn't want to see me again, and it doesn't matter which excuse she uses!"

Kassidy sighed, wondering why Millie hadn't mentioned the puppies to Warren the other night when they'd gone to the theater. Perhaps they'd been too busy talking about other things, she decided, keeping to herself Millie's excitement over their date when she'd run into Kassidy in the ladies' rest room the next morning. They'd had a simply marvelous time, the legal secretary had said. Exciting, romantic, and very, very special were all words she'd used repeatedly until Kassidy had gotten the idea.

Millie was in love.

"Maybe you should offer to help dog-sit," Kassidy suggested, feeling that was probably what Millie would hope she'd say.

"You think she'd let me?"

Kassidy tried not to laugh as she imagined Millie's response. Of course she'd let him. "You can only try," she said calmly. "Remember how persistent you had to be to get a date with her in the first place?"

"It was worth it, though," Warren said, his eyes going all soft and dreamy. "Millie's a girl in a million."

"And you're going to love the dogs, too," Kassidy told him. "All five of them."

"Five dogs?" he asked, a little frown marring his otherwise perfect features.

"Four-week-old golden retrievers, to be precise. She hired her little sister to watch them before and after school, but at all other times they have to stay in the bathroom. I'm sure you understand."

But Warren obviously didn't, and Kassidy didn't want to spoil things for him. How could she tell him that Millie hadn't yet devised a way to keep them confined to the kitchen where they wouldn't tear up anything important? On Sunday, Millie had gone to services for an hour and had returned to find five, very ambitious, golden retriever puppies teething on her newly reupholstered sofa.

"I guess I'll wander across the hall, then," Warren said, leaving his perch on Kassidy's desk without saying goodbye. She didn't mind. What with an enormous pile of paperwork and vacation just a few days away, she had enough to keep her busy. The telephone rang just as the market closed, and she was busy watching the day's final quotes flash across her computer screen as she answered it.

"I've got a surprise for you," Matt said. "Can you meet me downtown at three o'clock?"

Kassidy scribbled her signature on the first of several letters the secretary had typed, trying to figure out how she'd get through the pile and still meet Matt. No problem, she decided, eyeing the work on her desk. She'd work through as much as possible, then come in early tomorrow. She wrote down the address where they were to meet, but before she could ask why, Matt had already broken the connection.

Another surprise! Kassidy grinned at no one in particular as she lowered her eyes to the papers on her desk. It was so wonderful being back together with Matt, she mused, then pushed all thoughts of love and surprises to the back of her mind as she set to work.

MATT STOOD at the back of the gallery and watched the man walk out with the drawing. *His* drawing, dammit, and Kassidy hadn't even seen it!

"I told you that you were going to be a success," Kenneth said from behind him. "Your work hasn't been here two days, and you've already made your first sale!"

Matt stared at the gallery walls, looking at the charcoal drawings that were his and thinking it was all a dream because he couldn't possibly be as good as Kenneth insisted. Almost a year ago, Kenneth had come over to his house for a beer after a football game and seen the sketches Matt had done on his last camping trip and left out on the counter.

That was when it had all begun.

At first, Matt had thought Kenneth was putting him on, that he was simply flattering him. But Kenneth had been insistent, and had asked Matt to meet his partner at the gallery.

They both said Matt's drawings were unique, even exciting. They'd wanted to see more. Matt had done more, shown them to the partners, waited almost breathlessly as they studied the various drawings of the forest and the wildlife that lived there, drawings that captured the peace he found in the wilderness.

His work was rough in places, they'd said, just a little, nothing a few art classes and practice wouldn't cure. He'd followed their suggestions, all the while phasing himself out of the daily routine of the sporting goods store, spending his days learning, practicing, perfecting.

And now, a year later, they'd agreed it was time for the test. Kenneth had taken ten of the drawings, wanting enough to fill one wall. And on this second day of the small exhibition, the first one had sold. When Kenneth had called with the good news, Matt had been beside himself, so excited that he couldn't wait to share his success with Kassidy. The customer was picking it up at four, Kenneth had said. That was why Matt had asked Kassidy to meet him at three, to give her a chance to see it before it was taken away forever.

"I thought you said Kassidy was coming," Kenneth said.

"She was," he replied flatly. "I guess she couldn't make it." And before Kenneth could ask any more questions that he didn't want to answer, Matt shook his hand and thanked him for everything . . . his new career, for a start.

And then he left for home, because there was no use waiting for someone who wasn't going to come.

"I LOST TRACK OF TIME—" she said.

"It doesn't matter."

"I've been so busy getting ready for our vacation—"

"That's an excuse! You didn't want to come. You had to choose between me and your work, and you chose your work. I shouldn't have bothered to ask!"

"If I'd known it was important—"

"It wouldn't have made any difference! Don't you see? I can't trust you to put me first. I'll never be able to!"

Matt ran the imaginary dialogue through his mind, over and over again as he drove home from the gallery. It hurt that she hadn't come; he was angry because she hadn't fulfilled her part of the bargain. He wanted to lash out, use words that would inflict upon her some of the pain he was feeling.

"You said you'd try to be better!" he screamed in his *imagination.*

"I tried! I am trying! You can't expect miracles!" she cried.

"But I want miracles! I want to know you love me enough to come when you say you'll come, be there for me when I need you!"

Matt played through her excuses, practicing the words that would wound her the deepest, letting his anger feed upon itself until it was no longer an emotion.

It was the end.

TRAFFIC BLOCKED HER at every corner, frustrating her overwhelming need to be gone, to be home. She banged her fist on the steering wheel when the light turned yellow and then red, and because that idiot man in the car in front of her didn't try to leap across the intersection as she might have done, given the chance. She seethed inside and out, letting her frustration with the traffic distract her from her thoughts; it was easier to be mad at everyone else in the world than at herself.

But she was mad, furious that she could have let herself be so bloody stupid! The work on her desk hadn't been that critical, she knew, but she was so determined to get it done that she'd forgotten her promise, forgotten to even look up at the clock.

Kassidy leaned on her horn when the light changed, nosing across the intersection with only inches to spare between her car and the next. She couldn't afford to get caught at the same light again, not when she needed to go to Matt and try to convince him it wouldn't happen again!

She'd already been to the gallery, had seen his drawings on the wall, had met the man who knew more about Matt than she did herself.

"*If you'd only told me the truth!*"

"*That doesn't matter! I asked you to come and you didn't!*"

"*But I didn't know it was important!*"

"*You should have known!*"

Back and forth, as she waited in traffic, she imagined how it would be. Each and every feeble excuse, followed by the reply she knew he'd make. She tortured herself with the scene, wanting to inflict pain upon herself because in doing so she might alleviate his.

"*When you said you were working, I assumed you were at the store.*"

"*Because that's what you wanted to believe! Work is all that ever matters to you, and as long as I was putting in the hours, you were happy. I didn't need to tell you about the rest!*"

"*I would have been happy for you!*"

"*Not until I sold that first one,*" he threw back. "*Because until then I wasn't successful. There was no future in it.*"

The imaginary accusation hurt. It hurt, clear to the core, because Kassidy was very much afraid he might be right.

THE GRANDFATHER CLOCK struck five as she let herself into the house. Kassidy listened to the rhythmic tolling, remembering, for some reason she couldn't fathom, the afternoon they'd bought the clock. It had been a sunny day, much like today, but there the similarity ended. She'd been laughing that day, with Matt, the man who loved her more than she'd ever believed possible.

How could he possibly love her now?

Fighting back the tears because she knew he'd never forgive her and unable to find a single reason why he should, she carefully set her briefcase on the floor and went to look for him. The house was so quiet that someone else might have thought he wasn't there, but she knew better. Matt was there, she could feel it, just as she could feel the anger and disappointment that permeated the silence.

He was in the library. Over by the window, staring out into the slanted rays of the late-afternoon sun . . . ignoring her. It was worse than she'd imagined; she'd expected him to be angry, yelling and demanding answers. Why couldn't she manage for once to put him in front of her damned job?

It was worse because the hurt was deep.

Kassidy just stood there, a little way inside the doorway, waiting for him to turn, to say something that she could respond to, to give her a clue as to how they were going to patch things up this time. She felt so stupid, so incredibly stupid for having done this to him. To *them*.

"I know I'm supposed to say that I'm sorry, but I expect that's not enough, not this time," she said in a low voice that quavered despite her best efforts not to let it.

She waited, very still in the almost painful silence of the room, wishing she could just turn back the clock and have the opportunity to start all over again . . . frightened because she didn't know if she could do better, given a second chance. That was the thing that really scared her—not Matt's anger. But what if he gave up on her now, told her it was over, that they couldn't live together because she didn't try hard enough to change?

The possibility scared her to death.

"I need to explain some things to you, Kassidy."

She froze; it was even worse than she'd imagined. He was beyond anger. He acted as though . . . as though he was giving up. Because the guilt was nearly overwhelming, she couldn't interpret it any other way. He didn't turn to face her; he didn't want to even look at her, she knew. She didn't blame him.

Matt didn't turn from the window, didn't move a muscle. He couldn't look at her and tell her how close they'd come to losing it all.

It had been very close indeed. Matt swallowed, concentrated on taking deep, even breaths as he tried to explain. "I could tell you it didn't matter, but that's not the truth. I wanted you to see what I'd done, needed you to understand my goals, my dreams.

"When you didn't show up, I waited for you. I watched a man take something of mine out of my life. You should have been there, I thought. My wife—ex-wife, whatever—you should have known that I wanted to share it with you."

Kassidy felt the self-hatred burn deep inside, knew there were tears falling off her lashes, but didn't care. She'd hurt him, badly, and couldn't even promise she wouldn't do it again, because she didn't know that!

Matt turned at last, looked across the room to where she stood crying, but couldn't go to her, not yet. There was so much she didn't understand . . . so much *he* hadn't understood when he'd dreamed up this mad scheme to make her his again.

"I thought I hated you for a moment this afternoon," he said, hearing a curious note in his voice as though he couldn't believe the strength of his own emotions. "I came back here and waited for you, so I could tell you to get out. And I thought about how I was going to say the words, even considered leaving you a note in an empty house that was no longer your home.

"But the pain was too much, too deep, and all of a sudden I found myself wondering how on earth I'd manage without you, because I love you so very much, Kassidy."

And holding out his hand to her, he silently urged her to join him, waiting for what seemed an eternity before she took that first step. When the first step was followed by another and another, each one a little faster, each one bringing her to the spot where he waited, then he could breathe.

"I'm sorry," she said when their hands met. The tears were flowing faster now, because she didn't have to be brave any longer. He was giving her another chance, she realized, and she'd take it. No matter how stupid and bullheaded and blind she'd been in the past, there was nothing that would make her hurt him again. *Nothing!*

She followed him to the sofa, would have followed him anywhere, as long as she could be with him. He kept her hand, and she held onto his as though it was a lifeline.

"We almost lost it today," Matt said. "And it would have been all my fault."

"But *I* was the one who was late," she said, but he just shook his head.

"Being late had nothing to do with it," he said softly. "I was furious, because you couldn't take five minutes from your career to pay attention to mine. It was my career that was so damned important that I nearly sacrificed any chance we had at making this thing between us work. Not yours, mine!"

"Excuse me if I'm a little confused," Kassidy told him, searching his eyes for a hint of the madness that must be there. "I thought it was *my* job that made you crazy, not yours."

He smiled; now things were so simple. "Your job used to drive me nuts, because I had all this free time and you had none. Now that I'm doing something that I really love, I can understand why you work so hard."

"You want me to go back to the way I was?" she asked incredulously.

"Absolutely not!" He leaned forward to kiss her lips and comfort them both, because it was something he wanted to do. After a long interval, during which her tears dried in salty streaks on her cheeks, Matt withdrew a few inches and continued. "I don't want you to go back to working yourself into the ground. But I understand how important moderation is, especially since I find myself increasingly hardpressed to work reasonable hours."

She couldn't believe her ears, but wanted to, so she made him repeat his words. When he did, Kassidy let out a whoop of pent-up emotion and threw her arms around the man she loved.

"I'm still going to try to be better," she said between kisses, wanting so very much to be what he wanted her to be, needing to show him that she loved him more than anything in her life and that she'd really, really try to prove it to him.

"I know that, love."

"I am sorry about missing you at the gallery," she said after a long, lovely hug and kiss she felt right down to her toes. "The man that works there—"

"Kenneth, and he owns it," Matt interjected.

"Whoever. He told me all about 'the one that got away.'" Smiling tremulously into his shining eyes, she said, "I'm so incredibly proud of you, love. I always knew you were special."

"Now you're telling me you only love me for my art," he kidded, putting his arm around her shoulders so that when he leaned back against the cushions, she'd come with him.

"We'll see," she said slyly, resting her head against his chest. "How much did that guy pay for it?"

LATER, MUCH LATER, Kassidy got around to asking the practical questions. "Where do you work?"

Matt grinned. "I built a studio at the store. I thought the discipline of having to work at this would be easier if I got out of the house." Pushing her off his chest and onto the cool leather of the sofa, he teased, "Besides, I never knew when you were going to show up on my doorstep with that key of yours. I didn't want to get caught before I was certain it was going to work."

"So it works," she said with a smile, watching as he got up to stretch cramped muscles. "I took some time, looking at the ones in the gallery. You're better than I remembered!"

"Is that a compliment?"

"Only if you promise to let me have my pick of your work from now on. There are a few walls here that need some terribly expensive artwork hanging on them."

"Nothing like bringing your work home!" he quipped, delighted with her suggestion.

"I still can't believe you've kept it a secret all this time!" she groused, not a little displeased that he'd so cleverly hoodwinked her.

"It wasn't easy," he assured her, flicking on the light and laughing as she blinked owlishly in the sudden glare. "But enough about this. Let's go grab something to eat. Pizza, anyone?"

Grinning because she knew he hated pizza, she told him she'd settle for drive-thru burgers and fries. "And I have to call Kenneth before we go."

"What's Kenneth got to do with food?"

"He said that if we were still together tonight, he'd call the man who bought the drawing and arrange for us to go see it."

"Kenneth is a sucker for romance."

11

THE BACKPACK WAS BIG and bulky and heavy, and she didn't feel anything like those people in the ads—the ones with suntans and toothy smiles and packs every bit as large as her own but obviously filled with feathers, because hers was nothing to smile about! Gingerly descending the stairs to the front hall, Kassidy briefly considered what a sprained ankle would do to their trip, but rejected the impulse as unworthy. She'd suggested this trip, and now she'd just have to put up and like it.

"Get it all in?"

Kassidy whipped around, nearly wiping out Beethoven in the process. Matt winced at the near hit and tried to remember she hadn't done it on purpose. She just wasn't used to carrying several days' worth of food and clothing on her back.

She smiled brightly. "Of course I got it in. I'm efficient, remember?"

"Want me to carry that out to the car?"

"Think I can't?" she challenged.

"Just trying to be a gentleman." Matt did, however, jump over a pile of what looked like arctic gear to open the front door for her. "I thought we'd take your car."

"That's only because all this stuff won't fit in yours." She stared at the enormous volume of unfamiliar equipment scattered on the floor.

"There's that," he admitted with a chuckle. "But we're not taking all this. I was just sorting through the gear to find everything we need. Still, there's quite a bit that won't fit in my trunk."

"If you'd buy a real car instead of a toy, you wouldn't have this problem," she pointed out, wondering how he was going to take the news that her rusty bag of bolts would soon be replaced by a model similar to his.

"If you weren't coming, it would all fit." Sifting the assorted equipment into two piles, he continued. "Not that I'd be taking all of this, of course. But I'm glad we're taking your car. It's safer."

"Safer?" Hitching the increasingly heavy pack into a better groove on her shoulder, Kassidy watched as he grabbed a couple of duffel bags as well as his own pack.

"I'm pretty sure no one will steal it."

"As if you'd care," she threw at his back and followed him out the front door.

Matt didn't comment as he dropped his load beside the car and went back for a second. Kassidy pushed her own pack onto the back seat, not waiting for Matt to do it for her. Then she returned to the house, going into the kitchen to make sure the note she'd written for Lenore, their cleaning woman, was on the refrigerator. It was, and Kassidy took a moment to double-check the list, digging a pencil out of a nearby drawer to add another item.

Having a maid wasn't so bad, Kassidy decided as she penciled in instructions for Lenore to pick up the dry cleaning. In fact, things were working out quite nicely. Given the choice of spending more time with Matt, time she'd normally have spent cleaning, and saving a few bucks, there was no contest. Grinning because she knew her attitude had changed considerably since she'd moved back in with Matt, she added an emergency telephone number—underlining "Emergency" three times for emphasis—to the bottom of the page.

Satisfied the list was complete, she snagged the bag of cookies, her reward for sponsoring yet another marathon baking extravaganza, and munched on one as she walked back out to the car.

"I don't see how we're going to get all this stuff to the campsite," she said, surveying the pile of equipment that easily outweighed the car.

"I'll make a couple of trips," he said. "It's only a couple of miles, give or take, to the campsite from the parking lot. I thought you might appreciate the extra comforts."

Comfort was subject to personal definition, Kassidy knew. But considering the growing pile of equipment, this expedition might turn out better than she'd expected.

She wondered if there was a portable shower somewhere in there.

"ANOTHER HUNDRED YARDS, that's all honey. You can make it."

"Of course I can!" she gasped. "Sometime tomorrow. See you then."

Matt hid a grin, knowing Kassidy wasn't feeling particularly humorous about things right now. "Why don't you stop here?" he suggested instead. "I'll go ahead, drop my stuff and come back for you."

"*I can make it,*" she said through clenched teeth. "I'm just not as quick as you are."

Matt didn't think it would be diplomatic to point out they'd taken the better part of an hour getting this far. They'd hiked just over two miles, maybe two and a half, stopping every ten minutes for a break. He was concerned, but tried not to show it. He would never have brought her on this trip if he'd known she was so out of shape.

Kassidy smothered the agonized groan that was a direct result of the pack eating into her shoulders, rubbing the flesh until it was raw. Naturally, she knew her imagination was running rampant, painting vivid images of bloody shoulders, bloody feet...and a bloody temper. Fictitious images, she hoped. At least the bloody body parts were. The temper was unstable, at best.

Kassidy figured the least she could do was try to keep a rein on it. It wasn't Matt's fault. The rest was strictly a figment of an overactive imagination, the result of a sedentary existence—and the thing she'd sneaked into her pack that weighed more heavily upon her conscience than her back.

However, her back was complaining.

"So *this* is what you do when you disappear from town," she said, understanding even less than she had before. Where was the charm of walking miles over uneven terrain with the minimum of necessities in your pack, and freeze-dried food your only reward at the end of a long day?

"More or less." Matt waited for her beside the trail, snagging her hand in his to pull her the last few yards. "Usually, though, I don't set up a base camp. I just carry everything I need on my back and keep going."

Thinking of the weight of her own pack, Kassidy winced. "I can't imagine, I'm sure."

Matt laughed. "Probably not." But it didn't matter. He'd love Kassidy the rest of his life, whether she could relate to hiking and camping and generally communing with nature or not.

That wasn't one of the requirements for loving someone. A certain amount of sharing was essential. Subsuming two personas into one was nonsense.

"Are we there yet?" She had to ask, not knowing if she could convince her feet to walk another yard or foot.

"Almost." He pulled her off the path, slowly pushing ahead through the underbrush so that Kassidy could follow without having to blaze her own trail. "Two minutes and you're there."

"Thank God," she breathed.

At that point Kassidy knew she was incapable of calculating the season, much less the time of day. Swearing she was going to join the predawn aerobics class at the office, she grabbed a swinging branch before it smacked her in the face and plodded on.

When Matt stopped, she stopped. Grateful because she assumed this was another rest stop, she sank to the ground, leaning forward just a little because the pack was longer in the waist than she was. It didn't matter, though. Sitting was sitting, and if she had to tilt forward a bit, she didn't mind as long as her feet were anywhere but beneath her.

"How do you like it?"

Kassidy thought about telling him, but restrained herself. He sounded so proud. "Terrific."

Matt frowned, wondering why it sounded as though she was reviewing a movie she'd hated, but wouldn't say so because she knew the producer was standing nearby.

"We're here. You can take that pack off now," he said, swinging his own to the ground, then coming to help her with the unfamiliar fastenings. "And there's a tree stump about ten feet away that might be more comfortable."

"We're here?" Her spirits rose, and she looked around the clearing with a better attitude. Leaving the pack behind, she took Matt's hand and allowed him to pull her up.

"Are you that tired, love?" he asked softly, wondering if this was the biggest miscalculation of his life.

"Course not," she puffed. "Must be the altitude."

"Of course," he agreed. "It's at least a hundred feet above Seattle here."

"There you have it!"

Once again, Matt kept his grin to himself. "I'm proud of you, love."

"What for?" But she knew, and she wasn't too ashamed of the accomplishment. She'd carried her own weight— figuratively, she admitted, although the pack had seemed to outweigh her at times—and she was still breathing.

Barely.

"For being such a good sport about all this." And then, if only because there was a bit of the devil in him, he added, "Now that I know you're so good at it, we can plan *more* trips." Smiling his enthusiasm, Matt said something more about not wandering from the clearing and left for another trip to the car.

She was alone. In the forest. With who knew how many wild animals and reptiles and other critters.

Kassidy was close to panic when a muffled, ringing noise reached her ears. Feeling as though she'd been rescued by the forefront of civilization, she frantically un-Velcroed her pack and dumped the contents onto the hard ground.

Again the cellular telephone rang stridently, calling her back to a life where people weren't at one with nature.

It was her secretary, wondering if Kassidy had remembered to sell Mr. Thompson's utilities bonds, and why the paperwork on her desk couldn't be found. The secretary said she'd been looking all morning and wanted to go to lunch.

Kassidy told her in three terse sentences where it was, that she'd told her this before, and that if she called again, it had damned well better be an emergency.

She'd just managed to tuck the phone into the bottom of her pack when Matt emerged from the forest with at least another ton of equipment.

Kassidy rushed to help him before something broke, thinking it might be something important...something like the bottle of wine she'd shoved into his pack when he wasn't looking.

"I COULD HAVE SWORN I packed dried peas."

Matt was sorting through the combined stores of food from both packs, studying each as though it might be the missing veggie. Kassidy lifted her eyebrows innocently, scanning the foil sacks in turn as she feigned an interest in his search.

The peas, she guessed, were at home, in her sock drawer. Along with the other things she'd displaced from her pack to make room for the phone. Maybe he wouldn't notice.

"I can't find the corn either!"

Then again, perhaps he would. "Maybe you forgot to pack them?"

Matt turned his attention from the pile to the intentionally innocent expression on her face. There was a clue to be found there, he knew. He just didn't know whether or not he wanted to find it. One thing he did know: Kassidy had deliberately omitted some of the food packets.

Maybe she was looking for an excuse to go out for dinner. Matt chuckled as a startled Kassidy stared back in confusion.

He decided to let her get away with it. "I guess we'll have our tuna sandwiches without peas, then," he said, and turned his attention back to organizing lunch. "Why don't you put our things in the tent?" he suggested, indicating the two-person dome he'd set up before tackling lunch.

Kassidy tried not to show her surprise when Matt didn't pursue the matter of the missing peas. She knew he knew, and he knew she knew he knew, and so on, but still he said nothing. Not knowing whether she should be on her guard or just grateful for small favors, Kassidy proceeded to do as she was told. Either way, she knew Matt wouldn't forget.

"How did you find this place?" she asked him over a mouthful of tuna without peas. "Is it in a guidebook or something?"

Matt smiled, enjoying her naiveté. "The path we used to come the first mile is probably in a guidebook. I wandered off that last time I was up here and found this little clearing. I'm pretty sure no one has been here since."

"How can you tell? Do you leave notes for each other?"

"There are signs," he said. "When I left, I scattered the rocks I used to support the butane stove. They're exactly where I left them." He pointed out the medium-size stones that lay around the clearing.

Kassidy was pretty sure he was putting her on, but decided to pretend she'd fallen for it. "You mentioned something about running water."

Matt nodded. "Not too far from here. There's a tiny waterfall, just tall enough to wash your hair if you're really careful."

"And you said we wouldn't have a shower!" she chortled, already looking forward to this unforeseen treat.

"It might be—" he started, cutting himself off before he ruined her pleasure. "A little cold," was what he'd meant to say, but she'd find that out for herself.

And he would be there to warm her.

"I THINK I'm getting the hang of this." Kassidy dug her toes into the precise place where Matt's larger foot had left an imprint in the earth, surging forward to catch up with him as he crested the rise. It was a steep hill, but she had followed instructions to the letter and found herself enjoying the climb.

It hadn't been that way yesterday. Then she'd insisted on picking her own route. Not only had she managed to tumble backward every few steps, but she'd ended up at the wrong place, a mistake that had cost her an extra half hour, because she'd had to retrace her steps and follow Matt's better planned trail.

"I thought we were going walking, not climbing," she complained, ignoring her surroundings as she unlaced her boots. Wiggling her toes in the fresh air, she leaned back against Matt's knees and took a breather.

"We are, mostly. But sometimes you have to climb a little to get the really good views. This is one of them."

Kassidy opened her eyes to the panoramic vista beneath them and understood. From up here you could see it all. "I'll bet the view from that mountain is something!" she exclaimed, pointing to a rugged-looking, snowcapped peak in the distance.

"You'll never know," he teased. "If you think this little hill involved climbing, you'd never make it up that mountain."

Kassidy turned away from the majestic view to stare at a rather spectacular man. "You really don't mind, do you?"

"Mind what, honey?" he asked, a half grin on his face as he pulled a curl away from her eyes, holding it just for a moment to watch the blue-black highlights vibrate in the brilliant sunshine.

"You don't mind that I'm not good at this, do you?" She wasn't, Kassidy knew. Two days and nights were enough to judge by anyone's book, so they were both aware that she simply wasn't cut out for life on the trail.

"It doesn't matter," he said softly, threading his fingers among the warmed curls. "I told you that before we left. If you never want to do this again, I won't mind."

"Is it really that simple?"

"Camping?"

She punched him in the chest. "*Us*, silly. You know what I'm talking about."

"Tell me." He wanted to hear her say the words...tell him she'd stay with him forever, because the bad times were finally over and gone. She'd said them before, over and over again since that terrible afternoon when he'd almost lost her forever. Matt had spoken the words, too, trusting in them; they were, after all, the truth.

"We're going to make it...as a couple. You and me, Matt Hill and Kassidy Canyon."

"Tell me more," he urged, swallowing the emotion that welled from his heart. "Tell me why."

Kassidy puzzled for a few minutes, trying to find the answer behind all the solutions they'd arrived at, the something that was beneath the compromises, the concessions. "I think we've finally stopped fighting," she said, somewhat surprised.

"That's it?"

Kassidy deliberated a little, then restated her position. "I can't say it any better. We don't argue anymore."

"Yes, we do." Matt spread his thighs, pulling Kassidy until she lay with her back to his chest. "We argue all the time. About books, the maid... And remember this morning when you wanted to go down to a café on the highway for steak and eggs for breakfast, and I made you eat granola?"

"That wasn't an argument," she said loftily. "It was merely a difference of opinion."

"Which we resolved. You said you'd eat granola if we could have wine with supper tonight. We compromised."

"We should have had it last night," she grumbled. "When you found it. My aching body needed a little alcohol."

"You were so tired, you wouldn't have appreciated the taste of it. I don't believe in wasting good wine." Stroking his palm down her arm until he reached her fingers, he laced their hands together. "Besides, we're not talking about wine. You were about to explain to me that we don't argue anymore."

"Maybe argue is too strong a word. We disagree now and then, I guess—"

"That's putting it mildly," he interjected.

Kassidy decided now was a good time to let him have his way. If he wanted to call it arguing, that was fine with her. The last thing she wanted was to get into an argument about semantics. She lifted her lips to kiss his chin, then tucked her head back into the comfort of his shoulder. "So we still argue once in a while," she conceded, "but I don't feel like I want to hit you with something heavy anymore."

"Mmm." He didn't say anything more, just brought her hand to his mouth and took a little bite out of the soft pad of her thumb.

"That's all you have to say? Mmm?" Kassidy felt her heart speed up as he nibbled on her thumb.

He ignored her question, drawing her fingers one by one into his mouth, sucking each one lightly before releasing it.

Her heart accelerated to an insane rate. "I thought détente signaled the cessation of hostilities," she said, scooting sideways just a little, enough that she could watch as her fingers flicked open the buttons of his shirt. "As you pointed out, we still argue."

"But do you feel hostile?" he queried, tensing as her tongue reached out to moisten the nipple she'd exposed.

"Not a bit."

"Then I'd say it was working," he breathed, forgetting the slow seduction of her hands as he gave himself up to her determined assault.

"There's one thing I like about this camping stuff," she said in between strategic attacks on his weak points. He had a lot of those where Kassidy was concerned.

"What's that?" he managed to ask. How he could talk at all was a mystery, what with Kassidy's tongue doing those incredible things on his chest.

"I like making love to you in the sunshine. It feels different, like we're the only two people in the world."

"That's only if we don't get caught," he said roughly, pulling her head up from its downward path toward his belt. "I think a little discretion is called for, love. Why don't we wander over toward those trees?"

"You told me we were alone here," Kassidy complained, letting Matt pull her to her feet as she concentrated on unbuckling his belt. "At least, that's what you said yesterday, when you took advantage of me at the waterfall. Were you fibbing?"

"H-hardly," he stammered, backing away from her seeking fingers. "But we're a little exposed up here."

"That's what I'm working on," she teased. "Exposing you, that is. Come back here and take it like a man." Still, she followed his retreat, slowly, stalking Matt in bare feet.

Matt saw the convincing leer on her face, measured her determination as he continued backing off the summit. Another ten feet, he thought, and they'd be in a small hollow, out of sight from anyone except the odd hiker who might choose this particular hill to climb.

He decided to chance it. Not that he really had a choice, not with Kassidy.

He'd never had a choice with Kassidy. Loving Kassidy was like the daybreak—inevitable.

12

"I SAID I was dying for a hot bath, not a cold shower." Rubbing a towel over her sodden hair, Kassidy tried to remember to keep her tongue away from her clacking teeth.

"You thought I might have brought a tub along?" Dropping his own towel to the ground, he knelt beside Kassidy and took over drying her hair. She really was cold, he realized. It surprised him, because the sun was still high in the sky, its rays streaming warmly into the clearing beside the waterfall. But she wasn't used to all this, he conceded. She didn't realize how ideal the temperatures were. He edged closer, encircling her naked body with his own, kneeling with her between his thighs, his hands busy with the towel on her head.

"Oh, my, that feels good," she breathed, pushing her back harder against the heat of his chest.

"I always did think I had a flair for drying hair." He threw the towel aside, dragging his fingers through the curls until there were no more tangles.

Kassidy smiled and let him have his little joke. It was pure bliss, having his body so near to hers . . . especially now, when the panic was gone. No longer would she have to wonder how she would ever be able to live without him.

No longer did she have to imagine long, lonely nights with only her bad habits for company. Not that she'd totally eradicated those habits, she admitted. A few, yes. But the others, well, they'd learned to work around them. Just as Kassidy was learning to work around those funny little quirks of Matt's that used to drive her crazy.

She'd learned, the hard way, it seemed, that there was nothing important enough to keep her from loving Matt for the rest of her life.

"I love you, you know," she said softly, arching her neck as his fingers stroked her scalp in a sizzling, slow rhythm.

Matt stared down into the blue eyes that flirted with him, giving silent thanks that they were back together again. It was time for his confession.

"I planned it all, you know, with a little help from your mother." It was something he needed to get off his chest, particularly before she stumbled onto the truth for herself.

"My mother helped you plan this camping trip?"

"No. Your mother doesn't camp any better than you do."

"Then what are you talking about?" Kassidy was intrigued, not so much by the mention of her mother—who, bless her heart, had called to commiserate with Kassidy on her vacation plans—as by the revelation that Amanda spent much of her time talking with Matt.

Matt snagged a towel from a nearby tree branch where he'd draped it to dry and rubbed it briskly across her goose-pimpled skin. "Our reunion. Get-together. Whatever you want to call it. She even suggested the bit about disappearing for a while after I was sure you were interested."

"You let me wake up alone in a hotel room because my mother told you to go camping?" Kassidy couldn't believe it. "Keep in mind that if you say yes to that one, my mother is going to have a lot to answer for."

"She wasn't that involved with the details," he fibbed, deciding he'd take the blame for the cat; there was no sense in Kassidy becoming too angry with her mother. "It was just a general idea, to give you time to think about things, once I'd stirred you up a little."

"That appear-disappear routine was intentional?"

"Absolutely."

"You showed up at the hotel lounge that night to see me, not your friend, Jack?" she probed, twisting out of his arms, narrowing her eyes as she saw the resigned expression on his face.

"It seemed too good an opportunity to pass up."

"What else did she contribute to your little scheme?" Kassidy wrapped the towel closely around her shoulders, totally fascinated by the unfolding conspiracy. "Did she convince Andrew he had the flu, or was it your date she had to dissuade?"

"Neither. Mine stood me up. The fact that yours got sick was a stroke of good luck." He realized something very extraordinary was happening. Kassidy wasn't angry! She was interested, not mad; intrigued, not furious.

"At least the whole town wasn't in on it," she mumbled, still suspicious about Andrew's timely illness.

When Matt didn't rush in to reassure her, the truth hit her smack in the face. In all likelihood there were very few of their acquaintances who hadn't been involved. She should be angry, Kassidy told herself. Outraged. She'd been manipulated. She was no more than a pawn in a chess match, no better than a puppet on a string....

And he'd done it all because he loved her. Kassidy kept her smile to herself. He deserved to suffer a little.

"There's one more thing," he said, knowing that if he got away with this, he'd won it all. "The cat. That was my idea."

"The cat?" Raising an eyebrow, she remembered in excruciating detail the events of that night. Mostly it was the nearly unbearable sneezing that came to mind, that and the fact that Matt hadn't let her stay with him. "Of course," she said softly. "The cat."

"It was all my idea. Marla didn't have anything to do with it."

"Marla was in on this, too?" she asked, making her voice deceptively soft, as though she really didn't know. Naturally Marla was in on it. Everyone, it seemed, had had a part in this farce.

"She only had to pretend she'd found the cat."

"So I shouldn't take her head off."

"If you're going to take off anyone's head, I suppose it should be mine." Uncomfortably aware of his vulnerable position and not really trusting Kassidy not to do something physically stressful to his body, Matt took a chance and shifted a little until he was sitting several feet away. Then, since he didn't really think he'd be pressing his luck, Matt told her the rest. "And your mother shouldn't be blamed for filling up the house so you couldn't go there. We didn't think you'd be safe to drive that far . . . not with your sneezing and all."

"You didn't, hmm?" Kassidy inched forward, fascinated as Matt, oh, so casually, moved an equal distance backward. She had plans for him, plans that he probably wouldn't approve of, but then, who cared what he thought? He was the slimeball who'd cornered her with the cat, and Kassidy was just about to get even.

Matt cleared his throat nervously and backed up another few inches until he was teetering on the edge of the freezing waters beneath the waterfall. "You realize, of course, why I couldn't let you stay at the house," he said, playing for time as he tried to figure a way out of the impending dunking.

Nothing came to mind.

"You were probably afraid you wouldn't be able to keep your hands off me," she said, letting him see the light of revenge in her eyes as she leaned forward and placed her palm firmly upon his chest. "I think the only question now is whether I'm going to push, or if you'll just jump in all by yourself, because believe me, you're not getting away with this scot-free!"

"But I brought us back together!" he pleaded, knowing he could take her with him if he wanted to, but deciding against it. That wouldn't do anything except get him into more trouble!

"That's indisputable," she agreed, getting ready to push. "But the cat idea was dirty poker, and you know it."

"It was your mother's idea!" he screamed. "It was your mother..." he repeated, as the freezing waters of the mountain pond closed over his face.

Kassidy waited until he'd resurfaced before she replied. "My mother wouldn't do anything so despicable, Matthew Hill. Shame on you for trying to shift the blame!" And with a smile on her face that bespoke her satisfaction at getting even, she spun on her heel and picked up her clothes in a frenzied hurry—before Matt decided that she needed to join him!

MATT TOOK HIS TIME drying off, shivering a little in the fading light as he used already damp towels to absorb as much of the moisture as possible before he pulled on his clothes. As he pulled his cutoff sweatshirt over his head, he thought he heard the far-off ringing of a telephone.

He was wrong, of course. The nearest phone was in Kassidy's car, nearly two miles away in the parking lot. He heard the sound again and smiled, content to discover his sense of hearing was unusually acute, crediting the clear, mountain air with carrying the noise so far, hoping Kassidy wouldn't make him run to the car in case the phone went on ringing.

Kassidy heard it, too, and panicked. Tearing across the clearing with her sweater half on, half off, she grabbed her pack and upended it, scrutinizing everything as the contents spilled out at her feet. On the fourth ring she spotted the phone and grabbed it. She was just switching it on when she saw the spider—precisely where she would put her mouth to talk.

Kassidy screamed, a brief, high note that stilled her hysteria, then threw the instrument to the ground and cringed as she watched the inchwide monster amble away across the pine needles.

Shaking a little, because she really disliked creepy-crawlies, she retrieved the phone and answered it. It wasn't working, she realized, and she held it out to check the On switch. In her panic, she'd disconnected the call before saying hello. Cursing her decision to bring the stupid thing in the first place, Kassidy threw it back into the pack, leaving the rest of her things scattered on the ground. Right now she was too rattled to care about picking them up.

Tugging at her sweater, she adjusted her clothes and decided it was just as well Matt hadn't been there when the call came. She wouldn't have to explain why she'd brought along a cellular phone. Not today, because she planned to ask Matt to marry her. Again.

She was formulating her speech as she dug through Matt's pack for the corkscrew, rehearsing it under her breath as she sorted through what was left of their rations. Hoping Matt would remember to bring the wine he'd left cooling in the pool, she plotted exactly how the evening would go. First the wine. Then a little food, a little more wine, and the stars overhead to add romance to the setting.

She'd never get a better chance, she knew. Maybe he'd say yes, because he figured he still owed her for the cat episode. Kassidy grinned, totally unrepentant about using whatever it took.

"You screamed?" Matt inquired as he pushed his way past a low-hanging aspen branch and into the clearing. He wasn't worried. After two days in the woods with Kassidy, he knew what her "creepy-crawly" scream sounded like.

"Spider," she said shortly, taking the wine he handed her.

"I had to leave the shampoo and soap at the waterfall. I'll go back for it later." The water bucket in his hand was full, sloshing onto the ground, a luxury, Kassidy understood, because people normally didn't carry galvanized buckets on camping trips—not when they hiked in. But Matt had thought she'd appreciate the convenience of not having everything poured out of a canteen, so he'd brought them up on his second trip from the car.

Kassidy was busy with the corkscrew, her fingers, for some reason, not cooperating with her mind. The cork refused to budge, and she was on the point of begging for Matt's handy intervention when the phone rang again.

She prayed for the interminable moment between rings that Matt wouldn't hear it. Foolishly, of course. Matt's ears were every bit as good as she'd feared.

"It's *not* your car," he said, staring hard at her backpack as the second ring pealed into the otherwise quiet afternoon. "It's your damned *pack*!"

Kassidy winced at his aggravated tone, lost between trying to ignore it on the off chance it would go away, and wanting to answer it. If it didn't stop ringing, she'd go mad.

In the end there wasn't much of a choice. It didn't disappear, nor did it stop ringing.

Without looking at Matt, she hunkered down in front of her pack and pulled the phone into the open. There, halfway into the tent, with the flaps billowing in a sudden breeze, surrounded by the clothes and miscellaneous items she'd not bothered to repack, she lifted the receiver.

Matt watched, all the joy suddenly gone from his day... from his life. She hadn't changed at all, he realized. Not even a little. He didn't listen to her words, didn't have to know what she said to the person on the other end.

It was enough that she couldn't let it go.

Matt wondered what the hell he'd do now without Kassidy in his life, wishing he didn't care. He was so angry with her for not trying harder. As if from far away, he realized she'd put the phone aside, that she was talking to him. So he listened, mostly because he couldn't avoid it.

"That was Gerald," she was saying. "He's having trouble with one of my accounts."

Matt just stood there, watching her in the failing light, his face impassive. Kassidy swallowed, knowing she'd committed an offense that was unpardonable. She had brought the cellular phone, had brought it because it hadn't seemed possible to stay out of touch with civilization, with her job.

"He's one of my biggest clients, and he called this afternoon wanting to get out of the market altogether, something about the Tokyo exchange plunging a couple thousand points last night, and he's afraid the same will happen to Wall Street." She knew she was babbling, because she didn't know how to get past the granite wall he'd erected in the time it took to answer one phone call. "The partners aren't advising any sell-offs, and Gerald tried to convince this guy not to panic, but he's being really stubborn, and Gerald . . ."

Matt tuned her out about then, not needing to hear any more.

He saw the panic in her eyes as she spoke, knew it was over. It hadn't worked. All their hopes for a future together were ruined. She'd be leaving now, and he'd help her. He heard only the hum of her voice as he began to make plans. It would take about fifteen minutes to break camp, but first he had to get her down the trail before the light was totally gone. She'd never make it otherwise, not in the dark.

"I told him to handle it."

He'd carry her pack, Matt decided, so they could move faster. And then he'd come back, maybe stay until Saturday. He could call from the ranger station to arrange a ride home.

Matt cleared his throat. "If you'll pack your things, we can get going."

"Where are we going?" Kassidy was trembling now, suddenly aware that her stupid mistake was going to cost her more than an argument about a telephone. It was going to cost her Matt!

"You've got to go back and resolve the crisis," he said evenly. "You'll lose the client. You don't want that to happen."

"I told you, I told Gerald! I'm not going back. He's just going to have to handle it by himself. Haven't you listened to a word I've said?" She was scared, shaking harder now as she tried to get through to him that she wasn't leaving!

"You're not going?"

"I'm not going," she said breathlessly.

"But you said . . . the phone—"

Kassidy just shook her head, smiling because it felt so incredibly good to know that for once she'd made the right decision. "I'm not going back. There's nothing I can do that Gerald can't. Either way, it doesn't matter."

"I thought you were leaving me," he said, the miracle of what she was saying finally taking hold. "I really thought you'd let your career come between us again."

"I was wrong to bring the telephone, but—"

"But you're still learning," he said gently, crossing to her, touching her to make sure she was real, holding her and letting her know he'd never let her go.

"I'll switch it off," she said. "I don't need it anymore."

"I know."

"I'll never leave you," she said softly. "That—" she said, and pointed to the phone "—that's my career. You're my life."

She wrapped her arms around his neck so that she could feel the beat of his heart when she laid her head upon his chest.

"I love you, Matt," she whispered, taking a deep breath as she felt his arms enclose her in his warm embrace. "I love you, and I want to marry you."

It seemed that she had to wait an eternity before he answered.

"I will."

It was like the storybooks. Kassidy lifted her lips to his, saw the stars, the moon . . . the man she loved more than anything. And he was kissing her. There were fireworks, rockets, bells and—

Bells! Frustrated and furious, Kassidy tore herself out of Matt's arms and stomped over to the telephone.

She switched it on, seething as she thought of at least a dozen insults she could shout into it, because she'd told Gerald not to call!

After a moment, and with as much aplomb as she could muster, she faced the man who stood in the middle of the clearing, the one with his fists clenched and a mean scowl creasing his brow.

"Matt?" she asked softly.

"What?" he growled, his clenched teeth preventing a real response.

"It's for you."

He said the first thing that came to mind. "I'm not home."

"It's Kenneth," she said with a little smile. "He's got some news for you."

Matt stubbornly refused to take the instrument from her hand. "How'd he get the number?" he snapped, curiosity starting to get the best of him when she didn't back off.

"I left it with Lenore," she said. And before he could use that to start a fight, she threw out a little bait. "Kenneth says he wants to talk to you about a showing in New York. Seems a gallery owner from there saw your pictures—"

Matt grabbed the phone. Kassidy smiled again, sharing his excitement as she turned away to look for the bottle of wine she'd dropped earlier. Finding it beside a camp chair, she sat down and made another attempt to uncork it.

They had more than one thing to celebrate tonight. Their engagement, Matt's first major showing—and tomorrow the camping trip would be over!

Kassidy gave up on the wine and went back to stand with Matt, melting into his strength as he put one arm around her shoulder and continued talking into the cellular phone.

Epilogue

"DO YOU SUPPOSE we're doing the right thing?" Kassidy twisted her napkin, a little nervous now.

Matt pulled his gaze from the window, sighing at Kassidy's attack of nerves. It had to be now, he wanted it now, but still, it seemed such a waste to spend a beautiful afternoon indoors when they could be outside, playing a carefree game of softball with those teenagers in the park across the street.

Except Kassidy would be watching, not playing. She didn't take very well to any form of exercise. But then, Kassidy had other interests.

Reaching across the table, Matt gently disengaged the embattled napkin and wrapped his fingers around hers to give her strength. "I think we're doing the right thing," he said. "But if you want to change your mind and call her . . ."

Kassidy nibbled at her bottom lip as she thought about the enormity of what they were about to do. "It's just that Mom will be disappointed," she said, lifting her eyes to Matt's and finding gentle amusement where there might have been exasperation. They'd been over this time and time again during the last few days.

"She thinks we're still camping," he pointed out. "Everyone thinks we're camping. We called them three days ago, when we went into town for additional supplies—"

"Which we wouldn't have needed if I hadn't gotten the insane notion I wanted to stay in the wilderness with you," she said, still a little bemused by her aberrant behavior. But she'd wanted to be with him for just a while longer, away from everyone and everything. And that lonely campsite in the middle of nowhere was awfully attractive when you were sharing it with the man you loved.

"And we told them we'd be gone another four or five days—"

"Madness," Kassidy muttered, although it had surprised her when she'd actually begun to enjoy herself.

"And we agreed to get this over with, didn't we?" he reminded her.

"But still, it's so sudden."

"We're just mending an error." His voice was firmer now as he grew more insistent. "Besides, who wants to come to another wedding?"

Kassidy grinned wryly. "I would have done it three days ago, if that clerk hadn't been so bullheaded about the waiting period," she admitted.

"Don't blame the clerk," Matt chided. "There is such a thing as state law." There were still fifteen minutes to wait before their appointment with the judge, and until she was truly his again, he knew he wouldn't relax.

Kassidy fingered the splash of orchids that Matt had pinned into her hair in an attempt to make her jeans and hiking boots a little more festive. It looked ridiculous, but it didn't matter.

Nothing mattered today, nothing—except what they were about to do. Grubby and a little bedraggled after six days in the woods, they'd not even bothered to stop at the house to clean up. That had been out of the question, because then they'd arrive too late, and neither of them could wait another day until they were married. Again.

They'd planned on waiting until the next morning, but suddenly, on the drive back into town, they'd gotten this brilliant idea.

And they certainly didn't have time to invite anyone.

"I love you," he murmured, leaning forward so the pair of lawyers at the next table in the courthouse's cafeteria wouldn't hear. "I'll never, ever, let you go again."

"We'll fight," she warned him, swallowing hard. She was still afraid he'd change his mind and they'd walk back out into the sunshine only to go their separate ways. But she had to remind him of the pitfalls, the things that had destroyed them the first time around.

It was his last chance to run.

"We'll fight," he agreed. "But not like before. We've learned, we've changed."

She smiled at him, sapphire eyes twinkling with a hint of tears. He loved to see her smile, especially today, with so much ahead of them to be happy about. And she was happy, he could feel it.

It was the kind of feeling that you knew was right, a firm trust in the future. Their future.

"We've learned," she murmured. "We're not perfect, but we've learned." And then, a little louder, because she wanted witnesses to this and the two lawyers sitting at the next table would be ideal, "I want you to promise me something, though."

"Anything, love," he agreed, knowing that he'd give her the world if it were possible. But she wasn't about to ask for that; the hint of mischief in her eyes told him she was after something far less substantial.

"I want you to promise me you won't allow anyone to take pictures of the ceremony."

"You think camping chic won't impress the grandchildren?" he kidded, noting the muffled laughter coming from across the aisle.

"Of course not. I just don't want to have to argue with our own children about what they will wear when they're married. Can you imagine the example we're setting for future generations?"

"I like that idea," he said, softly now; this was for her ears alone.

"A tradition of camping chic?" she asked, suddenly a bit worried that he'd hired a photographer, after all.

"Children," he said. "Grandchildren. It has a nice ring to it."

Kassidy agreed, then looked up to find a white-haired man in flowing robes motioning toward them from the cafeteria doorway. "Speaking of rings, here comes the judge."

"Shall we do it, then?" Matt rose to his feet, holding out his hand, trying to hide his impatience.

"This time it's forever, Matt," she promised, rising onto her toes to plant a light kiss on his lips. "I won't give you up again, no matter how crazy you make me."

"Whatever it takes, Kassidy," he murmured, tucking her hand into the crook of his arm as they crossed the room to join the judge. "To keep you, I'll do whatever it takes. Forever is only the first step."

And then, because they wanted to get a start on forever, they hastened their steps toward their new beginning.

HARLEQUIN *Temptation*

Lovers Apart

**FOUR
CONTROVERSIAL
STORIES!
FOUR
DYNAMITE
AUTHORS!**

Don't miss the LOVERS APART miniseries—four special Temptation books. Look for the third book and the subsequent titles listed below:

March: **Title #340
MAKING IT by Elise Title**

Hannah and Marc . . . Can a newlywed yuppie couple—both partners having demanding careers—find ''time'' for love?

April: **Title #344
YOUR PLACE OR MINE by Vicki Lewis Thompson**

Lila and Bill . . . A divorcée and a widower share a shipboard romance but they're too set in their ways to survive on land!

HARLEQUIN
Romance

This March, travel to Australia with Harlequin Romance's FIRST CLASS title #3110 FAIR TRIAL by Elizabeth Duke.

They came from two different worlds.

Although she'd grown up with a privileged background, Australian lawyer Tanya Barrington had worked hard to gain her qualifications and establish a successful career.

It was unfortunate that she and arrogant barrister Simon Devlin had to work together on a case. He had no time for wealthy socialites, he quickly informed her. Or for women who didn't feel at home in the bush where he lived at every available opportunity. And where he had Tanya meet him to discuss the case.

Their clashes were inevitable—but their attractions to each other was certainly undeniable....

You'll flip . . . your pages won't!
Read paperbacks *hands-free* with

Book Mate • I

The perfect "mate" for all your romance paperbacks

Traveling • Vacationing • At Work • In Bed • Studying
• Cooking • Eating

Perfect size for all standard paperbacks, this wonderful invention makes reading a pure pleasure! Ingenious design holds paperback books OPEN and FLAT so even wind can't ruffle pages — leaves your hands free to do other things. Reinforced, wipe-clean vinyl-covered holder flexes to let you turn pages without undoing the strap . . . supports paperbacks so well, they have the strength of hardcovers!

Pages turn WITHOUT opening the strap

SEE-THROUGH STRAP

Reinforced back stays flat.

Built in bookmark

BOOK MARK

BACK COVER HOLDING STRIP

10" x 7¼", opened.
Snaps closed for easy carrying, too.

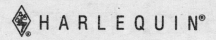

COMING IN 1991 FROM HARLEQUIN SUPERROMANCE:

THE·BYRNSIDE·INHERITANCE

Three abandoned orphans,
one missing heiress!

Dying millionaire Owen Byrnside receives an anonymous letter informing him that twenty-six years ago, his son, Christopher, fathered a daughter. The infant was abandoned at a foundling home that subsequently burned to the ground, destroying all records. Three young women could be Owen's long-lost granddaughter, and Owen is determined to track down each of them! Read their stories in

#434 HIGH STAKES (available January 1991)
#438 DARK WATERS (available February 1991)
#442 BRIGHT SECRETS (available March 1991)

Three exciting stories of intrigue and romance by veteran Superromance author Jane Silverwood.

SBRY

Everyone loves a spring wedding, and this April, Harlequin cordially invites you to read the most romantic wedding book of the year.

With This Ring

ONE WEDDING—FOUR LOVE STORIES FROM OUR MOST DISTINGUISHED HARLEQUIN AUTHORS:

BETHANY CAMPBELL
BARBARA DELINSKY
BOBBY HUTCHINSON
ANN McALLISTER

The church is booked, the reception arranged and the invitations mailed. All Diane Bauer and Nick Granatelli have to do is walk down the aisle. Little do they realize that the most cherished day of their lives will spark so many romantic notions....

Available wherever Harlequin books are sold.